ALSO BY BERNIE KEATING:

When America Does It Right
   AIIE Press, Atlanta, GA, 1978

Riding the Fence Lines: Riding the Fences That Define the Margins of Religious Tolerance
   BWD Publishing LLC, Toledo, OH, 2003

Buffalo Gap Frontier: Crazy Horse to NoWater to the Roundup
   Pine Hills Press, Sioux Falls, SD, 2008

1960's Decade of Dissent: The Way We Were
   AuthorHouse Publishing, Bloomington, IN, 2009

Songs and Recipes: For Macho Men Only
   AuthorHouse Publishing, Bloomington, IN, 2010

Rational Market Economics: A Compass for the Beginning Investor
   AuthorHouse Publishing, Bloomington, IN 2011

Music: Then and Now
   AuthorHouse Publishing, Bloomington, IN 2011

A Romp Thru Science: Plato and Einstein to Steve Jobs
   AuthorHouse Publishing, Bloomington, IN 2013

Riding My Horse: Growing up in Buffalo Gap
   AuthorHouse Publishing, Bloomington, IN 2013

Searching for God
   AuthorHouse Publishing, Bloomington, IN 2013

Chasing Tumbleweeds

A novel about turbulent teenage years

Bernie Keating

authorHOUSE®

AuthorHouse™ LLC
1663 Liberty Drive
Bloomington, IN 47403
www.authorhouse.com
Phone: 1-800-839-8640

Published by AuthorHouse   05/05/2014

ISBN: 978-1-4969-0980-0 (sc)
ISBN: 978-1-4969-0981-7 (hc)
ISBN: 978-1-4969-0979-4 (e)

TABLE OF CONTENTS

TO COLLEGE

Scott opened the cardboard suitcase and began to pack; pulling the wool shirts his mother had made off hangers and laying them atop the socks and underwear. It would be a rush to finish in time to catch the ten pm Greyhound bus at the Wyoming junction. The corduroy pants his mother had made may not be fashionable at college in Colorado, but they would have to do; he had no other. Anyway, he would become a midshipman in the U.S. Navy, narrowly avoiding being drafted, and could wear portions of his midshipman uniform to college classes.

On the dresser was the cowboy hat he found last summer working at the ranch; should that go with him? It'd probably be laughed at on campus. Cowboy boots sat on the floor in the corner, polished and looking new except for the rundown heels; certainly a vast improvement from the mud covered mess he found discarded in the bunk house. Sometimes they were important to wear because it gave him three inches in height. He had few dates in high school, but maybe in college he'd get the courage—or whatever it took—to ask coeds for dates. If they didn't like a guy who wore cowboy boots, then it was too bad; maybe he'd put the boots in a sack and carry with the suitcase. There were no girls in Edgemont he ever got excited about—and visa versa—perhaps college would be different; he hoped so: time for a new start.

Of course, it was different with Penny, but she was always going steady with some guy and never interested in Scott. They were good friends, but that was it—never did kiss or neck. He felt bad not saying good bye last night, even though she probably didn't care. Then there were his buddies, Jerome and Herman, but they had already left for college last week without saying good bye; were they really too busy to come see him? He missed Penny already even though she probably didn't miss him. He liked to sit on the stool at the Drug store and talk to her when she was working behind the fountain.

"Hello, Penny," Scott had said with a spirited voice as he climbed onto the stool in the otherwise empty drug store. "I missed you at the game tonight. Wished you were there. It was a good game."

"Yes, I know" she said and nodded indifferently as she wiped the shelf behind the counter, scarcely looking up. "Jim was in earlier and said your team won. Was it a good game?"

"Yeah, I guess", he replied, not knowing how to respond; it was his best game ever and he had made the winning basket—it didn't even register with her. How to start a genuine conversation with this girl? Maybe it was a lost cause: expressing feelings.

He tried to be out of the place before closing time when her boyfriend would arrive to walk her home. Scott wondered if she would have gone steady with him if he'd ever asked. Why hadn't he? Was it bashfulness or a lack of courage—unwilling to risk receiving a "no"?

There was no one else in Edgemont he would miss, other than family. He hoped to make some girl friends in college. It would be nice to have some true friends—someone he could feel close to. What he secretly wanted was affection, the warm feelings he could share with a girl and receive back. Pondering those confused teen years, he wondered if they were the normal seesaw process of growing up. Yes, there were some good times—real good—but why did they come intermixed with all the rest? Yeah, he was popular, got straight A's, was star of the football team, things like that; but why did it leave him feeling empty, unsatisfied? Why couldn't he ever have a steady girlfriend like other guys: Freddie Guynn, or Chub Bergen, or Ernie Dibble; or even date girls other than to take one home sometimes from a school dance? Walking home alone after one dance, he looked in the window of the drug store and saw Chub Bergen sitting in the booth with his date, Ethel, drinking cokes, laughing together, and having lots of fun. He took Wanda to a Saturday night dance one time, and it was boring talking and dancing with the same girl all night; she didn't act as if she liked it either. It was the first time he'd asked a girl for a date to a Saturday night dance and it was a disaster; she opened her front door, walked into her house, and didn't even say goodnight.

His dad and mother drove Scott to the Wyoming junction at the state line to catch the Greyhound bus. Mother seemed pensive and sad to see him leaving, but Dad was proud to see his son off to college; a chance he never had. Scott was happy to be leaving for a new life.

He gazed at the sagebrush prairie as it passed by outside the bus window and the landscape grew dim in the fading sunset, leaving his hometown far behind. Maybe the tumbleweeds swirling in the wind alongside the bus were an omen; time would scatter bad memories just like wind chasing tumbleweeds. The bus crossed the state line and headed to Cheyenne; he could feel the moment it stopped shaking on the rutted road of South Dakota and settled down on the smooth highway of Wyoming. It would reach Cheyenne after midnight and then he'd catch another bus to the University in Colorado. He closed his eyes, but sleep would not come and thought again of that time four years ago when he moved to a new hometown.

* * * * * * * * * * * *

December 15, 1942: It was bitter cold with a blizzard looming when they pulled up to the house; the frigid winter had already started in October.

"Wow! Our new home," shouted Betty as she pointed to the gray stucco house. "I'll bet that bedroom window will be mine. Dad promised me I could have a bedroom by myself."

Mother waved out the driver's side window to signal to Alan Coats in the cattle truck to pull in behind. "Scott, get out of the car and tell Alan to back up to the front door. We'll unload our things through there. His tarp will protect the furniture from the snow."

"Whew," Scott moaned, buttoning his coat as he climbed out, "Dad warned us it wouldn't be a fancy, and he was right, it sure isn't. Look at that pile of rubbish piled against the back door. The yard looks like the city dump. If the house isn't on its last legs, it is getting awfully close, and I hope the roof doesn't cave in."

"Well remember kids," Scott's mother interjected quickly in a defensive voice, "what Dad said before we began this move; Edgemont is a wartime boom town. Every house in town is already occupied with people living any place with a roof overhead: in chicken coops, trailer houses, and even in tents. With a war going on, we're lucky to find a house with three bedrooms and a roof overhead. So let's all look at the bright side. Okay? Remember, a home is what a family makes of it. Okay! Even if it is a bit rundown, we will fix it up so it will be a good place to live. You can count on Dad and me for that."

The family was fortunate to find any house in Edgemont. It was a World War Two boom town created by the government. When the U.S. Army realized they had to build an ammunition depot to stockpile bombs and needed a place to do it, they chose a site near Edgemont. The ammunition depot was near this prairie town in the southwest corner of South Dakota. The deadly explosive weapons had to be stored for months ahead of the time when they would be needed to drop on Germany and Japan. Some of the bombs were the two ton variety that could demolish an entire town. The army needed a remote location where an accidental explosion would not wipe out too many people or raise too much havoc. Hundreds of concrete bunkers half-buried in the ground provided bomb storage. The isolated prairie landscape five miles south of Edgemont met the requirements; the town was about as remote and expendable as anywhere in the nation.

Edgemont, located alongside the Cheyenne River across from the Black Hills, existed because of the railroad passing through that operated from Omaha to Billings. Rolling prairie stretched toward the Nebraska state line that was fifteen miles to the south, and toward the Wyoming state line that was twenty miles to the west, and nothing occupied either space except cactus, sage brush, coyotes, rabbits, antelope, and a few cattle grazing on the sub-marginal land. It was a barren landscape that became even bleaker when a coating of snow covered the cheerless gray shale buttes during the frigid winter that began in October and lasted until May. The weather was brutal with temperatures of thirty-five below zero and rose to one-hundred-ten in the hot summer sun.

The town's population, which had never exceeded five hundred, struggled to keep food on the table during the years of the Great Depression. The local bank had closed its doors in 1930 following the Stock Market Crash. Railroad employees and ranchers were the only families assured of any income, and little of that. A third of the town's men were unemployed and worked on the WPA, Roosevelt's welfare program to provide gainful work by taking on small projects. Building outhouse toilets to replace those falling over was one of the WPA's projects, but the major one was to build a National Guard Armory next to the high school where army troops could be trained for war. After it was finished, virtually all the young men in town over 18 years of age became active in the National Guard and earned income by attending a weekly drill. After Pearl Harbor day when the United States was suddenly in war, the local National Guard troops were immediately called up to active duty and received orders to the West Coast for deployment in the Pacific. After that, the only use for the Armory was for local high school activities such as basketball. There were virtually no young men left living in Edgemont except for those in high school.

The nearby ordnance depot became an economic boon for the local area. Rather than rely entirely on the town of Edgemont to provide facilities for workers at the ordnance depot, the government decided instead to build a project town to house all the workers and their families. This new town arose like a phoenix from the sage brush prairie. Six-foot high woven wire fences were erected and armed guards patrolled the perimeter, and other fences separated bomb bunkers from the homes where people lived. A double woven wire fence topped with barbed wire separated a forbidden area where poison gas was rumored to be stored. Schools were built and teachers hired. Miss Ward, who had formerly been superintendent of the Buffalo Gap high school, was hired as superintendent of the newly built school and she hired George Bain as coach and Miss Hajek as elementary school principal, both of them from Buffalo Gap. A commissary was opened where local people could shop and buy groceries, a movie theatre was constructed, a recreation center was built where local kids could hang out, and gradually the government project became a real town. It needed a name, so by vote of local people it became named after the most visible object in its landscape, the hundreds of concrete bunkers dug into the prairie that looked like an Eskimo igloo when covered with snow: the town was named "Igloo".

Everyone going to the project filtered through Edgemont during the months Igloo was under construction. Workers came without their families and lived anyplace they could find with bed and a roof overhead. The war created a melting pot. Many hires were Sioux Indian families who came from the nearby Pine Ridge Indian Reservation where most had been unemployed for decades back to the time when they were wandering nomad tribes and herded by the U. S. Cavalry onto the reservation. For many of these Indians, the ordnance project was their first opportunity for paid work and an actual house to live in with modern facilities. As housing gradually became available, families moved out to their new homes in Igloo.

Scott's dad had helped to restart the bank in Edgemont that had been closed since the 1930 financial crash. He had been commuting after turning the Buffalo Gap bank over to Scott's mother to run. For some time they had wanted to end his commuting and move the entire family to Edgemont, but there was no place to live. Finally, a house came available because it fell into bankruptcy. Since the bank had clout, the house became available. The previous owner had hastily departed the area, so the county sheriff moved the belongings into the yard out the back door where they still remained.

A neighbor rancher in Buffalo Gap, Alan Coats, had volunteered his cattle truck with high sideboards as a moving van. In switching from cattle to household goods, he had hosed it out and made a tarp available for a top, which became necessary; halfway to Edgemont it started to snow and the swirling wind increased. The move into their new home would be accomplished during a blizzard.

Scott climbed out of the back seat and entered the empty house through the front door with his mother. "Well, it sure isn't pretty," he mumbled, "and it is colder inside than out. I wonder if that stove in the corner will work. I'll look out back and see if they have left any kindling or coal in that shed out there", he muttered as he pulled his coat collar up higher on his shoulders. "I'll try to get some heat in here."

With his mother, he walked into the kitchen that was empty except for a kerosene burner propped up on legs sitting in the corner. They stood at the only window looking out. The ground north of the house sloped downward to the Cheyenne River, which was lined here and there with scattered cottonwood trees. It was a dreary scene.

"Can't see much through the frosted window and swirling snow," his mother said.

Scott grimaced, "Not much to see anyway," he said cynically. "I guess those cottonwood trees line the banks of the Cheyenne. They call it a river, but an old feeble man could jump across the trickle of water".

"All this will look better once we get some heat in here," she suggested. "Scott, please go out back and see what kind of fuel you can find. Maybe there is something in that shed. Billy, go with Scott and give him some help."

He paused momentarily to take in the dreary scene. The snowstorm was increasing, but beyond the river through snowflakes he could make out the dim outlines of the foothills of the Black Hills. He was reminded of the Whittier's poem he had to memorize that described 'cheerless hills of grey' and 'sadder light than waning moon'. Was this cheerless landscape of Edgemont where he now had to live?

He and his little brother, Billy, made their way through the back door, which hung askew on its hinges, picked their way over a pile of snow covered rubbish, and went looking for a coal shed. There was no coal, but fortunately he found some burnable wood and soon had a fire started. Maybe the place would seem more inviting once it became warm.

His dad came home that evening from the bank to a heated house and the family even had chairs around a table and a few pieces of furniture in the front room. Mother managed to lite the oil burner and warmed a pot of stew for supper. The family left at seven in the evening for a high school basketball game in the Armory. Scott's big brother Edwin, who had started the school year in Edgemont, was already a member of the second team and left early to get dressed for the game. The family drove through the snow storm to the National Guard Armory, which was already packed by a noisy crowd that completely filled the bleachers that lined the basketball court. Taking a place in the bleachers, they saw Edwin in his basketball uniform sitting on the bench as a potential substitute. Even as a new student he had been able to make the second team.

Scott watched as the tall center on the Edgemont team, who was identified by the crowd as LaVern Harusha, sank a basket from mid-court moving his team ahead. It was a great shot. Scott's younger brother, Billy, raised his hand and yelled along with everyone else in the bleachers: "Yeah Harusha!" Billy had already found a new team and his new hero.

Scott wasn't so sure! He wasn't ready yet to accept life in this new town; it would be a drag. He'd wait and see. Monday would be his first day at the new high school and he did not know what to expect. It would be a nervous weekend.

2

NEW SCHOOL

"Scott, it's bitter cold outside," his father whispered, like it was a big secret, "and more than a little cold in here. We've got to warm things before the family gets up," His father gave Scott's shoulder a light tap to wake him up. "Would you go out to the shed in back and get another bucket of coal. The one from last night is all gone, and while you're at it, bring in some wood kindling for the kitchen stove."

Bernard Keating was the first out of bed on cold mornings and on his feet by six to get the day started. The bank opened at nine for customers, but there were a lot of things to do here at home and at the bank before it opened the doors; particularly here in the cold dilapidated house they had moved into.

"Gee, Dad, it's awfully early!"

"I know, but we've got to start early and get this place warmed up. Maybe we'll find a better stove, but right now we've got to use that old one left in the house."

"Is it snowing outside?"

"No, not yet," his Dad responded. "I suspect it's below zero. If it starts snowing later in the day it may even warm things up. In the meantime, we've got to make do with what we have."

"Edwin has already left to run to the bank," he announced, "to get it warmed up, and the sidewalks shoveled and ready for the customers when it opens. We need you here at home."

"Lucky Edwin," Scot murmured under his breath. "I'll bet he'll be happy after he gets drafted into the army!"

The family moved to Edgemont in mid-December, two weeks before Christmas. Already bitter cold, the winter had come early and a couple of inches of snow covered the ground. Deep car ruts in middle of the street were the only means of foot traffic; everyone walked in the ruts and stepped aside into deep snow if a car came, which was seldom.

After his dad awakened him he got out of bed and dressed in the frigid room he shared with his two brothers. If it was zero outside, it must be almost as cold inside in his bedroom. After starting a coal fire in the pot-bellied stove in the main room and another wood fire in the kitchen range, he bundled up with a heavy coat and stocking cap and waded through deep snow to the coal shed. A new load of coal had been delivered yesterday, so he loaded two buckets to last through the day and hauled them to the house. There was no kindling yet for the kitchen stove so he chopped some wooden lumber—broken chairs—left-over by the previous owners and carried it to the house and stacked in on the back porch. His nose and ears froze; the thermometer indicated it was five below zero. Some of the chill was gone inside the house when he sat down to a bowl of oatmeal cooked by his mother.

"Damn, it's cold out there," his brother Edwin announced as he walked through the back door on his return from the bank. "The bank was as cold as a well digger's nose in the Yukon."

"I didn't know they had well diggers in the Yukon," Scott challenged his older brother. "I thought they were gold diggers, and I heard it was their butts that froze?"

"Please, Boy's, it's too early for any of that," his mother interjected as she ladled a cup of oatmeal for Edwin and refilled Scott's bowl. "You'd better hurry to get ready for your first day of school. Scott, would you go wake Betty so she can start getting ready."

The day before on Sunday afternoon Scott had walked to see his new high school. It was better than the rundown red sandstone school in Buffalo Gap and twice the size. That one held both the high school and grade school together; the latter occupying the four rooms of the ground floor and the high school the four rooms on the top floor. An ornate and creaky wooden staircase led all the way down to an empty basement that held nothing until toilets with running water were added. Only two years earlier, they finally got indoor toilets to replace outhouses that stood on the open field behind the school. This high school here in Edgemont had its own two storied building and also a two story grade school next door. The huge National Guard Armory was located to the north and contained the basketball court, raised stage for performances and school plays, and dressing rooms for athletic teams were in the basement. Scott was impressed and thought the school buildings looked neat. He was able to peek in through the front door and see the stairs leading upward to the second floor.

Edwin, Billy, Betty, and Scott all sat in the kitchen elbow-to-elbow eating around the small table with barely room for two. Edwin was the only one who said much. He had been rooming with his dad with the Seppalas and attending classes in Edgemont since the first of the year when the Buffalo Gap high school closed. The rest were worrying about their first day in a new school. What would it be like? How would their teachers be? What kind of kids would they find? Would anyone in the school be friendly?

"I'm worried about my teacher", said Betty as she chewed on a mouthful of cereal. "I wonder if it will be a man or women. Miss Hajek was so nice and she never raised her voice, even when some of the kids were acting up."

"I hear there is a shortage of teachers, so who knows what we'll get. I saw that basketball coach Jackley at Friday's basketball game, and he didn't look all that friendly," observed Scott nervously. "He was even yelling at some of the players."

"I'll bet some of the girls will be snooty to newcomers like us," said Betty. "In Buffalo Gaps all the girls were so friendly, except to a few of those kids from out in the country."

"But Darrell Thompson was a bully," said Scott, "and I always had to be careful when I was around him except during recess when he was afraid to act up when other kids were there."

"Relax. I've been going to classes here in Edgemont for three months, and everyone has been friendly to me so far. It is no different than in Buffalo Gap, most everyone is friendly, but you will always have one or two skunks like Darrell Thompson in the woodpile. My teachers are like teachers always are; they just do their job, some better at it than others. The principle, Austen Wells, is nice and just like Mister Lovell in Buffalo Gap."

"Hush up, you kids," scolded their mother, "and finish your cereal or you will be late for school."

School started at nine. At eight-thirty, Scott headed out the front door by himself wearing a heavy coat, galoshes, and a stocking cap pulled down over his ears. Wading through six inches of snow, he hunched his shoulders and pulled the coat's collar higher around his neck to keep cold from creeping down the back. A tablet notebook and pencil was the only thing he carried since he did not have any text books. Maybe the school would supply them? No sidewalks were shoveled so he waded through the snow to the ruts in the middle of the street and started walking in them south on the way to school.

Normally a fast walker, this morning he trudged along in no hurry. What would he encounter inside that school house? He did not know anyone there; didn't know any students and not even the names of the teachers. What would they be like? Would they accept a new student, or would they be unfriendly and treat him like just another transient in a boom-town, or consider him an outsider? Anyway, he was rather shy and reserved even in Buffalo Gap where he knew everyone. He had never gone to a new school before; how did it work? What classes would he have to take and what would the teachers be like? Putting his head down and pulling a scarf up to protect his face from the cold and hutching his shoulders, he forged ahead with a cadence that revealed his uncertainty. His galoshes crunched against the frigid snow as he walked in the hardened rut in the middle of the street.

It was five blocks to school, two blocks south and three blocks west. He reached the intersection, turned west, and saw several students ahead walking in the same direction. They all wore heavy coats and galoshes and were walking on the partially cleared sidewalk, so he left the rut in the street and moved behind them to the sidewalk, walking carefully because it was slippery. Two girls reached the front steps of the school ahead of him and one held the door open so he could enter with them.

"Thank you," he said smiling.

"Are you the new student?" The tall, pretty one wearing a felt hat asked in a friendly voice.

"Yes, this is my first day of school. Can you tell my where the school office is."

"Well, Austen Wells is the principal, so I guess his office would be the school office," she said with a smile. "He is down the hall and to the right. I'll show you."

"Thank you," he responded and followed them down the entry hall. At the corner the girls pointed to the right as they turned left. They walked into a hall that was packed with students taking off coats and placing things in lockers. It was crowded and noisy. Scott turned right and saw an open door across the hall. A girl was leaving the office where a man sat behind a desk wearing a grey jacket.

Scott stood in the doorway. "I'm looking for the school office," he announced.

"You found it. Come in," the man announced in a friendly voice.

"I'm a new student. This is my first day of school."

"Good for you," the man said and smiled. "I am Austin Wells, the Principal. You must be Scott. We've been expecting you. Your dad came from the bank last week and registered you, so you are all set. Welcome to Edgemont High School. Pull up a chair, Scott, and I'll get you started. Take off your coat and put it on a chair and I'll get you assigned to a locker so you can put your coat and books there."

Already Scott was feeling better. The principal, Mister Wells, already knew his name and was expecting him. That was great, and his smile seemed friendly.

"Scott, here is a schedule of the classes your Dad signed you up for. Actually, every freshman takes the same courses, so there isn't much of any decision to make except for the optional last period when you can either go to the study hall, or take journalism, Latin, or the first half hour of basketball. Your Dad indicated Latin. So you will miss the first half hour of basketball, it's no big deal, you only miss the warm-up. You will still make the practice session." Scott didn't like missing the start of basketball practice, but didn't think he could object since it was his dad who had made the decision. The principal took him to a locker where Scott left his goulashes and coat, and led him into the large study hall that was filled with rows of desks.

"Scott, this will be your study room desk where you will go when not in class." The principal placed his hand on the shoulder of the boy hunched over a text book sitting in the desk ahead. "Jerome, this is Scott. He is a new student. He is a freshman like you and taking all the same classes, so would you please help him find all the rooms. Scott, classes start in five minutes at nine o'clock when the bell rings, so Jerome will help you find your classes. Thanks Jerome." Then Mister Wells left.

Jerome turned and looked back. "Hi Scott, our first class is algebra with Miss King. It is hard." Immediately the bell rang and he stood up. "We'd better go." Scott followed him up to the second floor, down the hall and into a room with the desks located on elevated tiers facing the teacher's desk and blackboard. It was the first time he had ever seen tiered platforms in a classroom where students had an unobstructed view of the blackboard; that was neat. Miss King, who was sitting, arose and walked over to the desk where he sat alongside Jerome.

"Hello, Scott, Austin Wells said you are a new student. We are glad to have you in our algebra class. If you will come up to the desk with me I will give you a copy of the algebra book. We have new books this year, so write your name on the inside covers." Then she walked to the blackboard to begin the class, wrote a formula on it, and started talking to the class. Jerome was correct, it was a difficult subject, but at least Scott was surviving the first day and already a student in Edgemont High School.

That afternoon after they completed the Latin class, Jerome and he left in a rush and ran to basketball practice in the Armory. "Scott, if you are like me, you will learn to hate Latin because it makes us late for basketball practice. Anyway, we only miss the warm-up drills and shooting baskets, and will always be on time for the scrimmage. I guess it doesn't matter too much because no freshman ever makes anything but the third team anyway." Jerome led him downstairs to the locker rooms and introduced him to the team student assistant. "Vern, this is Scott, he's new today so he will need uniform shorts, and a sweat suit."

"Sure thing, come over here and I'll fit you up. Do you have any basketball shoes?"

"No"

"Okay, we will loan you a pair from our stock of left-overs for use just for today. Then by tomorrow you will have to bring your own." After dressing into the uniform, Scott followed Jerome upstairs to the court where teams were already shooting baskets.

"Scott, you will be on the third team like me," announced Jerome, "so we'll shoot baskets on the side basket while the coach is working with the first and second teams on the court. When scrimmage starts, we'll probably be sitting on the bench. The coach will substitute us in from time to time so we will get to play part of the time. Coach Jackley is a very good coach."

Scott was awestruck with the beautiful basketball court. It was huge with a shining, highly polished hardwood floor, and all the out-of-bounds lines and free throw lanes marked in heavy black paint. He had never seen a more beautiful basketball floor, even in Hot Springs or Rapid City; it was great. In Buffalo Gap the high school team had to dress in the school basement and then run four blocks downtown to the Auditorium where all the basketball was played. It was a tiny court with coal stoves on two corners that stuck out onto the playing floor and the stoves were marked with lines around each to keep players from getting burned hot on winter days.

In Buffalo Gap grade school they had to play in the dirt field behind the school, and even the high school team often practiced there rather than run downtown to the Auditorium. Two poles were erected on each end with backboards and baskets. The dirt court sloped to the south that required an adjustment in shooting and was full of pebbles that caused the ball to be deflected when dribbling, so a guy learned to pass rather than depend on dribbling, and had to use a heavy hand to get the ball to bounce-up off the dirt. Scott was the best player in the Buffalo Gap grade school and managed to make baskets even during windy days. He had never played inside on a real basketball floor like this one in the National Guard Armory.

After taking some practice shooting, the scrimmage started. He sat on the sideline bench with Jerome and the other guys on the third squad watching the play between the first and second teams. After a half hour, the Coach Jackley blew his whistle and told one guy to sit down and signaled Scott to come to the floor. This was it, his first chance with the team and first time on a hardwood floor.

"Scott, welcome to the team," the coach said. "Have you played basketball before?"

"Yes, Coach, last year in the 8th grade, but Buffalo Gap did not have basketball this year, so I only got to play on an outdoor dirt court behind the school."

"Okay, today you will play a right forward position on the orange team. He waved his hand and the play resumed. Only a minute into the scrimmage as Scott was coming forward out of the back court, a hard pass came in his direction but he managed to catch it and dribbled to the right center of the court. Suddenly there was no one guarding him.

Someone—maybe it was the coach—yelled "shoot". There was no wind to consider or sloping basket, so he planted his feet and aimed for the backboard just above the basket and took a shot. Wow! It bounced off the backboard, rolled twice around the rim, and then dropped in.

"Nice shot," Coach Jackley yelled!

Scott already loved Edgemont! Could it ever get any better than this?

FURLOUGH

The train from the east coast into Rapid City was on time. Mother and Scott stood on the platform and watched as the Pullman car slowly came to a stop.

"Denis!" he shouted and waved to the sailor who looked out from the train window. "There he is in that second car." Scott pointed him out to his mother, as if she would not recognize her oldest son, even thought he was wearing a navy uniform. Denis saw them and waved, then disappeared to reappear moments later standing on the Pullman platform. He waved again and clambered down carrying a duffle bag with the assistance of the conductor.

Scott rushed forward. Denis held out his hand for a handshake, but Scott flung arms around Denis's waist in an embrace. This was his big brother—a hero—no handshake could convey the thrill he felt in seeing him again after the two years he was in combat at sea serving his country. This man with the petty officer stripes on his shoulder and combat ribbons on his breast was his big brother.

Denis dropped his duffel bag on the ground and threw his arms around his mother in a long embrace. She had tears in her eyes, and maybe he did too.

"Mother, it's good to be home," he said with his voice breaking-up— he had seldom felt such emotion before. "I've really been looking forward to getting home and seeing all of you again."

"And we're sure happy to have you safely home," she said wiping her eyes with a handkerchief. "Dad and the other kids can't wait for you to get back home to Edgemont."

"Edgemont?" he said in shocked response, then remembered that his family had moved. "That's right; Edgemont is now my new home, isn't it?"

"Yeah, Denis, it is," Scott replied. "At least I guess it is—that's where we live—but Buffalo Gap will always be sort of hometown for me. Denis, is it true like the paper said, that your aircraft carrier, the USS Guadalcanal, was under attack by a bunch of German U boats and almost torpedoed?"

"Yeah, but Scott, I can't say much about that. We've all been ordered to keep a tight lip. Like they say in the navy these days: loose lips sink ships. So I can't really say where we've been or what we've been doing, but Scott, we spend a lot of time at sea and usually I don't even know exactly where we are. I just hope the Captain and Navigator know. Anyway, it's great to be headed to home."

Scott picked up the duffel bag and they walked through the depot and out onto the sidewalk. "We are parked across the street," Mother announced, pointing to the green Chevrolet. "We are still driving the same car, the green 37 Chevy, and I guess we will be driving it until the war is over; there probably isn't a car in the entire state of South Dakota less than four years old. Detroit is making tanks not cars. Scott, you carry the duffel bag and put it in the trunk." They crossed the street and climbed into the car.

"Denis, here are the keys. You are still the official driver, so take over. Oh, but the new national wartime rules are a maximum speed limit of thirty five miles per hour."

"Thirty five, that doesn't sound much different than the speed limit Dad always placed on me. At least now he has an excuse when he says, 'Denis, slow down, you're going too fast'".

They all laughed. "Yes," his mother said, "and we are also driving on retread tires that will have to last us until after the war because there are no new rubber tires anywhere, and we have to save gas because the ration stamps seem to run out before the end of every month."

Denis climbed in the driver's seat and headed out of town. Mother and Scott had driven the four hours from Edgemont to Rapid City this morning to meet the train bringing Denis from the East Coast for his first furlough in over two years. The rest the family couldn't come because Dad was needed at the bank and Betty and Billy were in school. Edwin had already joined the navy rather than waiting to be drafted into the army. Scott had begun to drive shortly before moving from Buffalo Gap, so Mother let him drive to Rapid City and kept a close eye on her fourteen year old son, ready to remind him whenever his foot got too heavy on the gas pedal. They had saved enough gas ration stamps by not driving anywhere for a month to make the trip, and a neighbor had loaned a ration book to buy gas since they seldom used their own car.

"Denis, what do you do aboard ship?" Scott queried his brother.

"I'm a first class electrician, which is the petty officer patch on my arm. That means I can do almost anything electrical aboard ship. I spend a lot of time in the engine rooms working on the electrical networks down below deck. I'd rather be topside, which is more pleasant, but I'm needed down there where there is a lot of electrical work. It is an unpleasant place, dark, cramped, and noisy, and hard to get around, particularly when we are underway in rough seas." Denis shoved his cap back on his head, hesitating. "I can handle the usual ship rolling and pitching, but when the sea is extra rough and we crank it up to thirty five knots to launch or take planes aboard, then sometimes I have to hang on to stay on my feet. When the ship is pitching forward and riding over high waves, the bow will pitch over a swell, the stern rises pushing the bow down, and suddenly the front of the ship goes under water; it's like slamming on the brakes. If it catches you unawares, it can send you crashing against a bulkhead."

"Denis, what are those ribbons for on your uniform?"

"Scott, not much of anything or medals for bravery if that's what you mean. They are for being in various combat zones and things like that. The top ribbon is a unit presidential citation for our ship engaging with a German U-boat, but I can't tell you much about that. It's still classified secret."

"Denis, did you hear that Tubby Bondurant was killed in action on Iwo Jima?"

"Yeah, I heard all about that in a letter from his sister, Helen, the army nurse. She is stationed in Tunisia. Tubby joined the Seabees because his bad legs kept him out of the navy. He was killed on Iwo Jima while driving a bulldozer against a Jap bunker. Just like Tubby to do something crazy like that." Denis paused as he pulled the car around a sharp corner. "Remember the time when he broke his ankle riding a bronco in the Buffalo Gap Rodeo, and that night at the big dance in the Auditorium he was trying to dance with a cast on his ankle. Tubby was always doing something crazy like that." Denis gave a short laugh, and then they were silent. "And I also heard that Jay McCrae was missing in action when the submarine he was serving on in the Pacific was sunk," he said during a momentary lull. "Buffalo Gap is getting more than its share of gold stars hanging in the windows."

They all fell silent and his Mother stared pensively ahead as Denis drove the car south in the direction of Hermosa. The gold stars hanging in the windows of parents in Buffalo Gap were all for young men killed in the war she had known from the time they were born.

"Denis, when you are out at sea in the North Atlantic and surrounded by German U boat wolf packs do you feel scared?" Scott queried, knowing it was time to change the subject.

"Probably not, because I don't even know they are there. I hope the captain and the sonar people and the depth charge people know they are there, but I am down below doing my electrical work, and I don't know what is going on around the ship. Sometimes we are at general quarters during an attack and one of my stations is on a forty MM gun on the fantail, but we never see anything to shot at. There are no enemy planes or boats, and the U boats are always submerged under the water. Destroyers are crisscrossing like crazy and dropping depth charges with under water explosions everywhere. Oftentimes we hear loud explosions when some liberty ship gets torpedoed and we pick up survivors from lifeboats. It can be a real mess."

We were all silent for a while until Denis asked. "Mother, I never hear from Edwin, but I suppose you do? Last I heard from him he was in boot camp at the Navy Pier in Chicago and about to board a troop train headed to some ship in the Pacific. What do you hear from him?"

"The news is sketchy. We got a postcard from San Francisco and apparently he was going aboard some ship, but wasn't permitted to tell us much. So we don't know where he is."

"That's odd," Denis said after some hesitation. "Who knows what is going on; he's probably okay. I hope the ship he's on has to refuel in Pearl Harbor so he can soak up some of that Hawaii sunshine. Maybe he can mail a letter from there. I wish my ship was in the Pacific instead of the North Atlantic where all we ever get is fog and bitter cold. Then, when we do get to port, it is some crummy place like Norfolk."

They were traveling through Hill City to Custer. It had snowed the day before and this road would be plowed clear. Highway #79 through

Hot Springs and Buffalo Gap would be shorter, but that road would still be impassable today. Denis was a good driver, and Mother relaxed with her oldest son behind the wheel. Scott sat in the backseat looking out the window. On the Minnehaha shortcut the car started to wobble and he knew immediately that it was a flat tire. After driving with a worn set of retread tires, Scott was skilled at changing flat tires and could do the job of changing a flat in less than a half hour if the spare was ready and did not need to be pumped up. He changed the tire to save Denis getting his uniform dirty. The family seldom took a trip anywhere but that changing a flat tire was not in the routine, what with retread tires, rutted dirt roads, and nails everywhere.

As they approached Edgemont, Mother realized she needed to get Denis prepared to see their new home, which probably would come as a shock to him after living in their lovely home in Buffalo Gap.

"Denis, we were lucky to find a home in Edgemont with all the houses already taken and virtually none available for anybody. Our home is entirely adequate, but you'd better get prepared to accept the fact that it is not as nice as our last one in Buffalo Gap. Okay?"

"Sure, Mother, I've heard all about it. Of course, if we still lived in Buffalo Gap, Dad probably wouldn't even have a job, because I hear nothing is left in Buffalo Gap since the war started except for a few ranches. Irene Swallow wrote me and said most all the people are gone and there is nobody left living there under the age of fifty—all old people and most of them ranchers. I know all about Edgemont and Igloo being like living in a wartime project. So, I'm not expecting any Rockefeller mansion."

As they approached town, Mother began giving directions. "After you cross the bridge over the Cheyenne River, take a right on the highway and go five blocks and then left," said mother. "I'll tell you where to turn." Denis followed directions and pulled in alongside the house.

"Mother, I see you've got your wartime emblem hanging in the window with the two blue stars for Edwin and me. Which one of the stars is for me, and which one for Edwin?"

"I never gave it any thought. We've never differentiated between any of our children. But since you are the oldest, I'll let you pick."

"Mother, I'll pick the blue star on the right side, because it is closest to the front door, and Edwin can have the one closest to the back porch.

Then he can carry in the coal buckets and take out the garbage when he gets home again from the navy."

"Welcome home, Denis," Scott declared. It was the start of a wonderful two week furlough at home with his hero.

THANKS AWFULLY

"Oh Richard, I love you," she said as she wrapped her arms around Scott and pulled him closer in a tightening embrace. He was petrified. Doris Sanders, a senior and the prettiest girl in high school, placed her mouth over his in a passionate kiss. Scott was so shaken that he forgot where they were.

The curtains had opened and the entire town was watching the opening scene of the high school play, *Thanks Awfully*. The shocked audience loved what they saw and gave roaring applause.

Scott was only a freshman and being kissed by Doris Sanders, a senior and most popular girl in school. In the hallways of Edgemont High School, senior girls would not even acknowledge the existence of a freshman like him, let alone speak to one. Nevertheless, in the tradition of "the show must go on", she was giving a performance that would make Hollywood proud. When the male lead of the high school play became ill yesterday, only a day before the performance, the director faced the decision whether to cancel the play or find a replacement on very short notice. There were few available candidates and they all turned down the part, inasmuch as they saw it only as an opportunity for a last minute public disaster. In desperation the director, Miss Uhl, turned her attention to Scott, the new freshman boy. He was tall for a freshman—as tall as Doris, which was a physical requirement for the co-star. Even more important, the director needed someone who was smart enough to learn the dialogue of a one-act play in only one day, and Scott fit that bill. Even as a new freshman he had gained the reputation as a smart kid. The challenge was not as difficult as it might seem at first glance, because ninety percent of the dialogue consisted of repeating the same line over-and-over again: "THANKS AWFULLY". How could anyone not master that task?

"Scott, you can do it. You'd be perfect in the part," encouraged Miss Uhl, the director and sponsor of the Thespian Club. "I'll help you learn the dialogue. It will be easy because you only have to learn one line and then just keep repeating it over-and-over again. Each time you will say it with a different meaning and inflection in reaction to what the other cast members say, but I'll help you with that part. Please, Scott," she pleaded, "the Thespian Club needs you and Edgemont High School needs you to step in and help us out of this sudden crisis. Otherwise we'll have to cancel the play. What do you say?"

Realistically, how could he respond? It was blackmail! Miss Uhl was also his English teacher and history teacher, and he needed all the help he could get for grades in those classes.

"Okay, Miss Uhl, I'll do it, but can I read the script first before I give a final answer?"

"Surely, here is a copy of the script," she responded as she handed him a sheaf of papers. "You'll see your parts of the dialogue are one liner's, and it is the rest of the cast who do all almost all the talking and they already know their lines. They will all be able to help you." That seemed to settle the matter and he knew it was a done-deal.

Then he read the script and went into shock! The play began with an intimate love scene between him and Doris Sanders. Wow! Scott had never embraced a girl up close like that before, let alone kisses on the lips—and now to do it with Doris Sanders—a senior who was a cheerleader, very beautiful, and the most popular girl in high school. He was too shy for that sort of stuff—it would be embarrassing and more than he had bargained for or could handle. Then he read the final scene where he had to go through that same embracing and kissing and love-making stuff with Doris Sanders all over again. Damn! Was it already too late to back out?

Miss Uhl excused him from afternoon English class to study and learn the script. The dress rehearsal was that night, only hours away. The director had underlined all his lines with clues for the inflection to be used for all the different "*Thanks* awfully." It was never genuine thanks, but rather a questioning one, or one for emphasis, a negative rejection, or an explanation—all sorts of things. He could get through that part okay.

At the dress rehearsal that evening, Miss Uhl helped Doris and Scott to gently embrace for the opening scene. He was terrified! They both seemed flustered and barely touched as they approached each other. Doris appeared to be embarrassed with her arms around a freshman, and Scott was a dozen degrees beyond nervous. His face felt flushed and his heart was beating so fast he got dizzy and thought he might faint. Miss Uhl recognized his anxiety and diverted attention to other things. She realized she could work on that opening scene of the play later after they became more comfortable with each other.

Then the story-line of the play unfolded. The star, Richard Montague, played by Scott, hated women and thought they were stupid. He bet his sister that he could get though one of her house parties and use only two words—no more than that—because he thought all girls are superficial and dumb and don't know how to carry on a conversation.

As the curtain opens, his ex-girlfriend and he are in an embrace when she tells him she is moving on in life and leaving him, but with a final hug, she gives him a goodbye kiss, and then departs. As his sister's party begins, the lady guests arrive chatting and they all go for the handsome brother of the hostess, who was Richard.

"Oh Sara. Is this your handsome brother?"

"Yes, Sally, Richard is my brother, but he's been away at school."

"Oh Richard, I'm so happy to make your acquaintance," she said extending her hand with a laced glove that extended nearly to her elbow. "And you simply must come to the party next week that I'm holding at the Metropole. Richard, my dear, you are so fetching and will be the life of the party."

"Thanks awfully," Scott responded with as much enthusiasm as he could muster.

"Ruth, please meet my brother Richard," his sister said turning to the tall skinny blonde with the big, oversized chest who had just entered. "He has been away in school at the Academy and just this week got back in town."

"Charmed," she said extending her hand and at the same time taking his elbow and pulling him close to encase him in double enceinte. "Oh Richard, I am delighted to meet you. You and I must really get together so we can talk about some mutual friends we have at the Academy. I insist you must come to my garden party on Friday. Richard, your sister has told me so much about you and you are the life of every party," she gushed unabashedly.

"Thanks awfully", he replied tentatively, happy he did not have to attend any party on Friday.

He continued to get along well using only two words "Thanks Awfully" and was able to repeat it with various inflections and meanings in an appropriate response to the party girls with all their chattering and shallow, meaningless conversation.

In a final scene his ex-girlfriend reappears, declares she changed her mind and is back again and still in love with him. In a climatic embrace, she promises her undying love and he exclaims, "Thanks Awfully!", and as the curtain slowly closes, she falls into his arms in an impassioned embrace and smothers him with fervent kisses.

As the curtain closed during the dress rehearsal, a new problem was revealed to Scott. There was a sudden and noticeable bulge in the crouch of his pants as his sexual urge was awakened with the intimacy of this beautiful girl in his arms. As he released her, he became aware of the visible protuberance in front of his trousers that all the cast members could obviously see. He blushed and stood in an awkward stance to minimize the exposure and hide his embarrassment.

"That was an excellent run through for a dress rehearsal," announced Miss Uhl to the cast, clapping her hands and attempting to divert attention away from Scott and his co-star. "You all did a fine job, and Scott, I'll work with you tomorrow on a different inflection for some of the phrases; but you did an excellent job with only four hours advance notice. The audience is going to love the play. Remember, everyone here tomorrow night for makeup at six-thirty, and then into your costumes."

He walked off the stage wondering how to handle that bulge problem. He played basketball in uniform briefs in front of crowds with no problem wearing only an athletic jockey strap under team shorts, but this was a different problem. Holding a beautiful girl in an embrace and kissing her and being kissed in return; he had no experience in how to handle that kind of problem. He'd have to think about what to do.

Before leaving home for the performance the following night, he came up with the solution: wear two pairs of tightly fitting jersey shorts under a tight jockey strap, and wear a loose pair of pants that camouflaged any problem.

For the performance that night, he was the star of the school play, *Thanks Awfully*. He may have walked stiffly with constricted tight hips, but he was like a crusader knight wearing a coat of armor. This was his night of "amour".

The play was a hit, and he remembered all his lines. In the final scene as he and Doris were fervently kissing and locked in a passionate embrace, the curtains slowly closed. The crowd roared approval with a standing ovation and were still standing even after the curtains had drawn closed. Miss Uhl gave the signal to reopen them again for a final bow and then the curtains closed again for a second time. The cast rushed from the wings to tell Doris and Scott the play was a smashing success.

It was then he realized for the first time that he kind of liked being kissed by Doris Sanders.

IGLOO

Don't look for it on any map, but there was once a city in South Dakota with a population of four thousand people named Igloo whose existence was during the years of World War Two. Its name came from the bomb cellars built into prairie sod that resembled the snow hut of Eskimos when covered with snow during the bitter cold of a Dakota winter.

And Igloo was a real town, too, with over four thousand people, schools, churches, hospital, grocery store, recreation center, and a movie theater; all these enclosed behind a six foot steel woven wire fence where a badge worn by every inhabitant with their picture was required for entry. Federal officers rode the fence line in jeeps, armed with a 38 sidearm and shotguns.

Scott's Uncle Clarence was visiting from Newell to see the new Edgemont home of his sister, and the family had just finished lunch when a loud distant explosion was accompanied with a sudden shaking that rattled the dishes on the side table.

"My God!" Clarence exclaimed, "what was that?"

"Oh, think nothing of it," Scott's mother announced to her elderly brother. "It's only the blast of a defective bomb being taken care of in the detonation area out in Igloo. That explosion was heavier than many, so it must have been one of the two-ton variety," she responded casually as if it was a routine event, which it was.

"You mean, that goes on all the time—those explosions?

"No, not all the time but several time a week. They've got hundreds of cellars full of bombs at Igloo and some of them turn defective and must be destroyed; so, they take them to the detonation area with blast barricades and blow them up"

"Wow! Ethel, how do you live with that?"

"Like everyone else here in town. There is a war going on and it's one of the things that have to be done."

"Well, I'm glad I still live on my ranch at Newell where the only explosions I ever hear are from one of my milk cows with an occasional fart."

When World War Two arrived the nation's ammunition factories were making bombs at a breakneck speed and the army needed a place to stockpile all these explosives; bombs had to manufactured and ready in advance of D Day for the allied invasion of Hitler's Germany. The prairie sage brush country five miles from Edgemont in the southwest corner of South Dakota was converted overnight into a huge ammunition depot. Two hundred concrete bunkers buried halfway into the ground became the home to thousands of bombs racked in stacks twenty feet high. Each bomb needed to be rotated by workers called ammunition handlers every month to remain viable. During the time this army base was being built, the nearby Edgemont became a boom town and grew over night from a population of a few hundred ranchers, merchants, and railroaders to over ten thousand who were mostly temporary construction workers. They occupied every building and shack; they slept in plywood trailer houses, tents and cars. A meal in a restaurant meant a long wait. The queue to cash a payroll check in the bank extended out the side door and around the corner. Sidewalks were jammed at night like in a carnival, and many ranchers who had survived the lean years of the Great Depression parked their cars on downtown streets just to watch the crowds on the sidewalks and admire the signs of a new prosperity.

"Howdy, Ed, good to see you and Grace," Tom announced as he rolled down his pickup window to talk to the rancher that had pulled into the sidewalk alongside. "Quite a sight isn't it, this busy town? Did you ever expect to see the day?"

"Ug! I guess so, but it doesn't do much for the cost of feeding my cattle," retorted Ed, who was not thrilled to be in town and would not be here except for his wife, Sara, who got lonely all the time in the country with no neighbors. "I guess it's what happens in wartime, but I don't remember anything like it during the last war."

"Say Ed, Sara says to ask Grace why you two don't drop over some Sunday after church for a chicken dinner. I'll check with the government," he chuckled, "but I don't think we are required to use any food ration stamps to kill our own Chicken."

"Sure thing, Tom, sounds good and I think we have enough gas ration stamps from the government for our pickup so we won't have to walk," he said laughing.

They watched as a drunk staggered along the sidewalk in front of their cars. With a dozen new bars in Edgemont, it was a common sight. Saloons played to packed houses: the Western, Buzz Beiber's Igloo Bar, the Liberty, Wagon Wheel, Jimmy the Greek's, The Silver Dollar, Al Kazmerick's saloon, and biggest of all was Hank Gordon's Stockman's bar, café, lounge, and second floor dance hall. Scott had a classmate whose mother worked as a barmaid in Hank's bar; she was attractive with a great figure and long blonde hair, and Hank kept her stationed at the window near the front of the bar as a lure. Another of Scott's classmates, Chub Bergen, had a father who worked as a card dealer in the back room of Buzz Beiber's Igloo bar. In addition to running an illegal gambling operation, Buzz also recruited some girls from Deadwood's brothels on the second floor above his bar, but it was short-lived because they were chased out of town by the local womenfolk: the town was "wide open"—but the mothers determined that had its limits.

At the same time that concrete bomb bunkers were being dug into the sagebrush flats, other workers were constructing the infrastructure of a government community: barracks, duplexes, Quonset huts, churches, grade school, high school, PX, a recreation center, and movie theater, plus streets and sidewalks.

Because of the labor shortage with all the young men younger than eighteen years drafted into in the army—unless they enlisted in the navy or marines first—there was work available at Igloo for anyone with minimal qualifications. For a man who had been working on the WPA or CCC during the depression years, these new jobs were a godsend. Some of the best jobs paid $2.00 per hour and since they sometimes worked ten hour days and weekends, a worker could take home $125 each week, many ten times his previous wages on the WPA. Government recruiters went to the Pine Ridge Indian Reservation and recruited Indians to leave the reservation and move to Igloo where they lived in newly built modern duplexes with running water and flush toilets. For some Indians this was their first opportunity to move from the abject poverty of living in shacks on the reservation where they had been herded by the U.S. Cavalry sixty years before. For many of these Sioux Indians it was also the first time they had lived in close proximity to Whites, and visa-versa and Igloo became a social melting-pot experience.

The government built a multi-denominational church, and Scott helped celebrate the first Mass there as an altar boy with Father Groell from Edgemont. The Catholic Mass was completed on Sunday morning at 9:30, the altar stripped, and then thirty minutes later a Protestant Minister moved to the podium and started services.

Jobs were available also for high school students over the age of fifteen. Scott and Jerome spent one summer building concrete sidewalks in front of new duplexes in the community, the following summer as skilled roofers placing temporary roof shelters on stilts over explosives, and another summer sand blasting rust from the fins of bombs.

The government project in Igloo had no on-site bank, so Scott's father and mother spent one day each week on the project operating a mobile bank under armed guards that moved from bunker-to-bunker to cash payroll checks for the ammunition handlers and government workers. The necessary currency had arrived by train from the Federal Reserve Bank in Omaha and was placed in the Edgemont post office safe. Scott's dad carried it from the post office to the bank in bulging bags under each arm, and he never owned or carried a gun. On the day for the Igloo bank operation, Scott's father and Mother were met at the bank door by uniformed army personnel who cleared the street, and carried shotguns. The U.S. Army was not going to let an armed robbery happen on their watch.

When the homes and infrastructure were ready, everyone moved in and the new town was named Igloo. Then the trainloads of bombs arrived and were stacked in the bunker cellars. Despite the unusual product handled by the workers, Igloo gradually became a normal town where children went to school, to the movie on Saturday night and to church on Sunday. The Edgemont High School basketball team played in Igloo often, and a traditional rivalry developed between the two towns, both of which were the same size and located only six miles apart. Igloo had excellent schools with the best facilities and equipment that the federal government could buy on short notice during a war. Tom Brokaw of later TV fame started his schooling in the Igloo grade school with the same first grade teacher, Miss Hajek, that Scott had several years previously in Buffalo Gap. It was an isolated community, but nobody noticed because those were the war years. Gas, tires, sugar, meat; it seemed everything was rationed.

Then during one month the crews were loading bombs out of the storage bunkers into railroad cars with shipments round-the-clock, headed to eastern ports. Everyone knew that D day and the invasion of Europe was at hand. Many workers had an army brother, or husband, or son in England waiting to go ashore; so few complained of the long hours and hard work: it was a time of high emotion.

Everyone anticipated that when the war ended, the base would be closed and dismantled. The workers would all be discharged and their family's belongings packed and moved elsewhere, to who knows where? Many were Sioux Indian families who would move back to their meager existence on the Pine Ridge Reservation from where they had come only a couple years before. The base would be dismantled; the buildings all torn down; the movie theater, church, school, and commissary would all disappear; and all the barracks and family duplexes disposed of. Alas! Even the sidewalks Scott and Jerome had crawled on their hands and knees to build would be bulldozed. At last there would be nothing left except for the concrete igloo bunkers that covered the empty prairie. That is the harsh reality of war. The prairie would return to sage brush, and coyotes moved back to reclaim their territory.

The history of the West is full of places like Igloo. In 1876, a boom town encampment of ten thousand Indians sprung to life on the banks of the Little Big Horn, where tribes of Sioux, Cheyenne, and others came together in flight from their common enemy, the White man. This Indian city of buffalo-hide teepees stretched for three miles alongside the river. Then General Custer leading the Seventh U.S. Cavalry attacked the village of Indians, and his command was wiped out. The Indians knew this meant bigger trouble ahead. Overnight they pulled down their teepees, loaded their meager possessions on the travois dragged behind ponies, and scattered to the winds. Within hours there was nothing left beside the river or on the bluffs, except for the carcasses of dead soldiers and coyotes. Some of the elderly warriors from sixty years before who had been at the Battle of Little Big Horn, had now been living with their offspring in Igloo duplexes. This was another ghost town, forgotten to history.

Nothing was left on the sage brush prairie landscape except for the hundreds of empty igloo cellars that dot the prairie to the horizon and coyotes hunting across the landscape. Historians may ponder what an archaeologist of the third millennium might think when they excavate this site: in the bitter cold in this remote forgotten region of North America, were these the igloos of the legendary Eskimo tribe?

6

DIGGING DITCH

"Hello," said Scott grabbing for the phone after realizing it had rung three times; a ringing phone was a rare occurrence in their household—no one ever called, so his ears were not used to reacting to the sound.

"Scott, Dad!"

"Yes, Dad, why are you calling?"

"Say Scott, a guy from the U.S. Geologic survey was just here in the bank to open an account," his father announced. "He is doing some government surveying work for the next few weeks over west in Wyoming and asked me if I knew where he could find a couple high school guys free for the summer to be his chain gang. I suggested you and your friend, Jerome. He said to have you contact him at his trailer house parked north of the highway."

"God! Dad," Scott exclaimed sharply, "what is a chain gang? That sounds sinister."

"Naugh. I worked on one when I was a kid back in Custer with my cousin, Sylvester. You go out with the surveyor to carry a six foot rod marked in inches, and you hold it upright at some distance from the surveyor who sights along a transom instrument and records the reading. It's called a chain gang because sometimes they use a chain to measure distances. Jerome will carry a rod too. It involves a lot of walking, but it's more like fun than work."

"Yeah, that sounds okay and I sure need a summer job to make some spending money."

"I think a lot of other kids would like that job, so you should scurry over right now to his trailer house north of the highway this afternoon and ask for the job. You'd better hurry before some other kids get there. His name is Hank Walberg and just mention your dad at the bank suggested you come right over. Tell him you'd like the job and are ready to start work tomorrow."

With everyone over the age of eighteen already drafted into the army or volunteering for the navy or marines, there were summer jobs available for any willing teenager, and it was considered patriotic of them to work in support of the war effort. Nowhere was that more true than in Edgemont with the U. S. Army ammunition depot nearby.

Shortly after completing the freshman year of school, Scott got this summer job that gave him a paycheck. The desolate country west of the Wyoming State Line had never been surveyed from the time when General Custer came through in his expedition, sixty-five years earlier. It was rugged prairie country with sage brush, sharp sandstone buttes, deep ravines, and was populated with jack rabbits, coyotes, antelopes, and rattlesnakes. It was the headwaters of the Cheyenne and Little Missouri Rivers.

Jerome and Scott began working on the new job the next morning, riding with Hank Walberg in the government pickup over the dirt trail into the craggy terrain of the Wyoming Territory. That rugged country had never been surveyed by the U.S. Geologic Survey except by air.

Hank Walberg carried the transit on a tripod across his shoulder and the two boys carried their six foot long rods. They walked to the starting point atop a butte where Hark set up his tripod and mounted a transit on top to focus on some star and establish the exact starting location. Walberg peered intensely into the telescope and fiddled with the settings. Scott couldn't see any star in the bright daylight and was not convinced Hank saw anything either. Apparently Jerome felt the same.

"Hank, what are you looking at through that transit telescope?" Jerome asked quizzically. "I can't see any star in this bright sunlight. Is there really anything up there?"

Hank Walberg nodded, "Yep, there sure is, I'm looking right now at Polaris, the North Star. It is where it is supposed to be at precisely noon mountain standard time. Do you guys want to see it?"

Scott looked into the transit telescope. "I sure don't see anything. Are you sure I'm looking at the correct spot?

"Well, Scott, it is very difficult to see and it takes some training and I suppose some faith. At exactly twelve noon, the azimuth and elevation of Polaris is a known location. It can help you fix the exact spot of any place here on earth. Of course bright sunlight is difficult to see through, but if you focus long enough on the crosshairs you can see a faint blur exactly where it is supposed to be."

Scott looked again into the transit telescope and did not want to seem inept. "Oh yes," he announced, "I can see it now." He felt rather guilty since he wasn't sure he really saw it, but didn't want to challenge Hank Walberg's expertise.

"When I focus on Polaris precisely at noon," declared Walberg, "the elevation and Azimuth gives the exact position here on earth in longitude and latitude within a couple feet. Isn't that great?"

"Yeah, it sure is. I'll take your word for it, Hank, but to me it seems pretty far-fetched," responded Scott with amazement.

Walberg then asked Scott place his rod on a flat rod at this precise point and hold it vertical and steady. Then leaving Scott holding the rod, Hank and Jerome walked to a distant bluff where Scott was still visible, and Hank setup his tripod and took a bearing on the rod that Scott held on the butte a quarter mile away. Hank wrote some numbers and then waved to Scott to come hither. Keeping his tripod stationary while swinging the transit, Hank instructed Jerome to walk to a knoll a quarter mile further along in the desired direction. When Jerome arrived at the new place, Hank used the transit to record the bearing of Jerome's rod. In the meantime, Scott had caught up to Hank and together they walked past Jerome where Hank setup his tripod, and the process started over again. Using this leap-frog procedure, they covered twenty miles of surveying each day. Each day when completed, they drove back to Edgemont to spend the night.

Scott loved the job and did not consider it working. In Buffalo Gap he had taken long hikes in the nearby mountains with Betty and Billy for the fun of exploring new places. He was always fearful of rattlesnakes because his oldest brother, Denis, had been bitten and nearly died, but his dad had educated him in how to safely walk through rattlesnake territory. He wore boots that extended well above the ankles, avoided walking where he could not see the ground, and was always ready to react fast if he heard the telltale rattle of a nearby snake. Hiking through the desolate country was interesting because they often saw jack rabbits, coyotes, antelopes, deer, cougar tracks, and occasional fox.

The survey job was completed in six weeks. With the rest of the summer ahead and nothing to do, it could become a boring time. Again, Scott's dad had the answer. The phone rang.

"Scott, Dad!"

"Yes, Dad, why are you calling?"

"Say, Scott," his father announced, "Tom Rabe was just in the bank looking for someone to work for him this summer and asked if you might be available. He runs the City of Edgemont's water systems and things like that. I said you just finished a job working on a survey crew for the U.S. Geologic Survey and would probably be available. Tom complained at being shorthanded, what with all the new work created with the "boom town" atmosphere, and suggested you contact him if you are interested in the job. It pays fifty cents per hour. I suggest you walk right downtown this afternoon to his shop back of the city hall and tell him you'd like the job."

Tom Rabe ran the City of Edgemont's water and sewer systems, street lights, city dump, and was town marshal who ran the jail and maintained law and order. So Scott had a new job together with his friend, Jerome Colgan, whose dad was postmaster and his uncle the mayor. They were politically well connected as the banker's son, postmaster's son, and mayor's nephew, so they had the inside track; however, no other kids in town had ever previously applied for the job because it involved the hard work of digging ditch. Scott and Jerome became Tom Rabe's new two-man City of Edgemont crew. Because of their parent's high visibility in the community, Scott and Jerome were in the glare of the limelight, and under a lot of pressure for good performance.

Digging ditch was no "piece of cake." The work was about as hard as a grown man could normally perform, and that was why the job was still open and available—no grown man wanted to do it. Just the process of digging was difficult enough but was made doubly difficult because the baked gumbo soil in Edgemont was nearly as hard to penetrate as concrete when dry, and sticky as glue when wet.

The boy's first job assignment was to dig a trench down six feet deep and two feet wide at the curb in front of the Daum home to find the water main, and then dig a trench to the house to provide a new hook-up. All the water mains in Edgemont were buried six feet deep to prevent freezing in the below-zero weather of the winter. The town's water system had never been mapped, so it was Tom Rabe's best guess where water mains were located along the curb lines, which were seldom marked by a sidewalk. After the boys dug deep enough to find the water main, then Tom would drill a hole in the pipe, rig a connection, and start a new outlet. That was the easy part. Digging down to the water main was the real challenge, and Tom usually climbed in his pickup leaving the boys with shovels and picks to start with their job, and then he drove away.

Scott grabbed a shovel and began by placing his foot on it and pushing down to get it started into the ground. With the hardest push of his strong right leg on the shovel, the blade did not penetrate even a quarter inch into the ground; it was hard as concrete. After more attempts, he laid the shovel aside and used the pick. Apparently Rabe knew it would be needed. Scott began to swing the pick, dangling it wildly over his head then punching the ground with a violent force. This was better than the shovel; the pick penetrated two inches deep. Then the process became one of using the pick alternatively with the shovel to remove the dirt the pick had broken free.

As the hole got deeper, the dirt had to be thrown by shovel up over their heads to the top of the diggings into a pile alongside the trench. Throwing the dirt all the way up and out the ditch required almost as much exertion as digging. Jerome and Scott alternated turns and sweated profusely in the hot sun. Fortunately they had a water bag. In the late afternoon when Tom returned to see their progress, they were down four feet in a trench two feet wide and five feet long.

"Good job, boys," he said. "It is hard work digging in this dry Edgemont gumbo soil." Scott arched an eyebrow and looked at Jerome out of the corner of his eye—like Tom Rabe was telling them a secret— but he said nothing. "Sorry," muttered Rabe with a grimace, "We don't have any water available at this location to wet the soil and make it easier to dig. We are down four feet and tomorrow morning we will go the final two foot and see if we guessed correctly on the location and find the water main." Scott wondered what Tom meant by using the pronoun "we" since it was Jerome and he who did all the work, and the two of them would probably dig the final two foot tomorrow morning. Scott hoped the water main would be where Tom guessed it would be or else they would be digging laterally right and left forever to find it. This sure wasn't fun like on the survey crew, but at least it was a job and paid fifty cents per hour, four dollars a day. It would make their dad's happy and put some money in their pockets for the local movie theatre on Saturday night that cost twenty cents plus five cents for a bag of popcorn. Taken together with his morning janitorial job at the bank, he was rolling in money.

The next morning they began again with pick and shovel and were down nearly another foot. They saw the indications of the iron water main pipe and Scott swung the pick harder to clear out the soil around and under it. Suddenly he hit a loud thud. Something cracked and gave way. Damn, it was the sewer pipe and he had already opened a four inch diameter hole on top of it and broken clay pieces had fallen into the sewer pipe. What to do? They waited for the return of Tom. When he drove up in his pickup, Scott brought him up to date.

"Tom, I don't know what happened," Scott volunteered, "but when I was using the pick to loosen up the dirt around the water main, suddenly I heard this thud and a hole in some clay pipe under it appeared. I don't know what happened." Tom investigated and drew the obvious conclusion.

"Well boys, a sewer line is often located just under the water main so they can both be buried in the same trench. Scott, you made the ultimate mistake. With your pick you broke into the clay sewer pipe." Now Tom's pronoun had changed from 'we' when they were digging to 'you' when talking about the new sewer problem Scott had created.

"It is not a big thing," Tom chuckled, "Scott, jump down, reach your hand into that hole in the sewer and clean out the debris, then I'll put a patch on the hole and we'll start digging the trench into the house. You boys are doing a good job."

Scott jumped to the bottom of the trench and looked into the hole in the pipe. Already he could smell the foul odor coming up and contemplated the task of putting his hand into the sewer. What to do? It seemed he had no alternative but to do what Tom had said.

All the sewer lines in Edgemont flowed by gravity to a location below the Cheyenne River bridge where Cottonwood Creek flowed and the sewer emptied directly into the river. It was a gruesome, smelly place where no locals except Rabe and his crew ever visited.

Carefully Scott rolled up his sleeve, reached his arm into the hole, and felt around among all the 'particles' until he found the fragments of clay and removed them, along with other unidentified things he threw into the bottom of the trench. Then he climbed out and found Tom and Jerome laughing. He walked to the water bag and nearly emptied it dumping water over his hands. That night he washed carefully with soap and warm water a dozen times before eating his evening meal.

Edgemont's nightlife was wide open. As a result of the transient drifters, by late evening the town's bars and sidewalks were populated with numerous drunks and the resultant fights. The bouncer at the Stockman's bar, Joe Cotton, carried an iron club "enforcer" in his hip pocket and was not timid to bring it into action on some drunk's head when called to do so. The night Marshal, Heavy Sheldon, had to throw a half dozen drunks into jail on a normal night, often with the help of Joe Cotton. The jail was located behind the City Hall and consisted of one large padlocked chamber with a toilet stool in the corner and two locked inner cells that could hold a dozen prisoners crowded together.

One of Tom Rabe's duties was to open up the jail each morning, get the prisoners fed a breakfast, and then lead them to appear before Judge Caylor. The "judge" had been appointed the local justice of the peace by Mayor Pat Colgan. He sat at the head of the conference table each morning in the one-room City Hall to dispense Edgemont's brand of justice. The preferred procedure was to get prisoners to escape and disappear during the morning jaunt to Jimmy-the-Greek's bar and restaurant for breakfast. Since they had not yet been booked, they were still free and clear. There was little sense to levy fines against these transients because none of them had any money. If they remained in jail, the city incurred the continuing expense of their meals. Judge Caylor would often impose a deferred fine and potential hard-work assignment to motivate their early departure from Edgemont. Sometimes, Rabe would take a nod from the judge and slip the prisoner the price of a one-way bus ticket to Rapid City.

Many mornings before going off to dig ditches, Scott and Jerome would accompany Tom Rabe when he opened the padlock on the jail outer door and enter to see who the marshal had thrown in cells the night before. If the prisoners seemed tame and repentant enough, he would announce that his two deputies (Scott and Jerome) would escort them to Jimmy-the-Greeks for breakfast. Then he told them after they returned, they would have to appear before Judge Caylor to be booked and determine how much fine they would owe and how many days in jail they faced a "hard work" assignment. It did not take genius for them to see that their deputy escorts were two teenage unarmed boys. Tom did not suggest the prisoners promptly return for their trial. Scott carried the money to pay the breakfast bill, and he noticed that by the time the last prisoner had finished eating, the rest had already slipped out and would be seen no more in Edgemont.

The boy's next work assignment was using the shovel and hoe to cut weeds around the city reservoir. It was not hard work but boring because the weeds would grow back anyway in a couple weeks. The top of Reservoir Hill was covered with embedded small rocks, so a shovel wasn't well designed to cut them at the roots. Scott and Jerome were not highly motivated, but it was part of the job when Rabe had nothing else for them to do and certainly better than digging ditch. They were resting in the shade when they suddenly saw Tom Rabe's pickup come roaring up Reservoir Hill trailing a cloud of dust.

"Oh my God! Here comes Tom. Quick on your feet and make it look like we've been working," shouted Scott to Jerome who lay with his eyes closed. They rushed to pick up their shovels and be in the act of cutting weeds. Tom braked to a stop alongside the boys.

"Quick! Get in the pickup!" Rabe yelled excitedly, "We need you. They've got a forest fire up on Parker Peak toward Hot Springs." The boys were happy for the diversion because cutting weeds was boring work. They threw their shoves in the back and climbed in beside Tom, who swung the pickup around and roared off again in a cloud of dust down Reservoir Hill.

Edgemont had a volunteer fire department and most members were local business men who were normally too busy to be available to fight daytime fires. If the fires were out in the country, then the rancher volunteers could take care of those grass fires. Fires alongside the train tracks started by hot coals from the engine fire box were a common problem, and Edgemont gave them attention because it was a railroad town. It was not Tom Rabe's job to fight fires, but he was expected to step-in and handle whatever emergency might arise in town. He was "Mister Fix-It".

"We'll have to stop at the city shop and pick up some stuff," he hollered over the roar of the truck. "We'll need shovels, pails, and burlap sacks."

"Burlap sacks?" Scott said in a questioning tone; that didn't make sense.

"They're for slapping down the flames in a grass fire," Tom replied. "You have to fight with whatever you can carry up steep hills. If it is a grass fire, then wet burlap bags are better for getting at the flames and slapping them out; more effective even than slapping with the backside of shovels, and seldom is dirt available. I hope the fire only involves the grass because trees are a whole different matter."

They drove back to the city shed and grabbed shovels, burlap sacks, and canisters of water, then drove out of town on the highway over Gull Hill toward the Parker Peak area. A train track ran alongside the ranch where the Parker ranch was located, and no-doubt sparks from a coal-fired train caused the fire. The train to Deadwood ran this way every morning. In hot summers, train fires were a fairly common occurrence, but thankfully seldom involved a forest fire near Parker Peak. As they passed over the top of Gull Hill and approached the area of the fire, they could not see through the dense smoke, so Rabe pulled off the highway onto a dirt trail to the east through the McKnight ranch to approach the fire from its back side. They came to an impassable ravine where they parked and headed on foot up the foothills toward the peak carrying shovels, burlap sacks, and water canisters. Tom led the way in a rush and moved at a near trot.

"Whew! Tom, I'm out of breath and need a minute," shouted Jerome leaning against a tree. "Give me a minute and I'll catch up."

"Boys, we've got to stay together," responded Tom, who was a heavy smoker and clearly out of breath himself. "It might get dangerous up ahead near the flames and the smoke so heavy it will be difficult to see anything." He leaned against a tree for just an instant, panting, and then exclaimed, "Okay, boys, time to get moving on."

The climb became steeper and walking a struggle; Scott worked harder and breathed harder than he'd done since last year in football. The smoke became too heavy to see beyond a couple feet. Tom Rabe and Jerome disappeared from view in the smoke, and Scott was alone. He didn't know where the fire was coming from—he heard a roar on all sides and may be surrounded by it. Then he saw flames leaping high in the grass ahead of him and began slapping at them with his burlap bag. He was making progress and the line of fire was slowly contained. Suddenly a huge tongue of fire jumped out of the flames into his face. Springing backward he dropped the burlap bag and lost it. Using the back side of his shovel, he began slapping at the flames again. Then he found some loose shale at his feet and scooped it toward the flames. It seemed to work, and the fire line in front of him was slowly dying out; but the smoke became so heavy he had no idea where other fire might be or what had happened to Jerome and Tom. Wandering around to his right side in the direction he thought was north, he found other firefighters.

"Have you seen Tom Rabe?" he yelled. "I was with him but we got separated in the smoke."

"Well, you've done a good job; the fire is all out in the direction where you were fighting it," replied one of the guys Scot recognized as a local businessmen. "No, I haven't seen Tom, but it looks like the fire is all out, so he's probably headed back in the direction he came from. Where did he park his pickup? Are you one of his crew?"

"Yeah."

"You must be Scott, the banker's son. Your face is so black from smoke I hardly recognized you. I didn't know firefighting was something Tom Rabe and you city workers did."

"Well, when you work for Tom Rabe and the city of Edgemont, you might be doing anything: that's for sure." Scott asked him to point the direction to the south toward the McKnight ranch where their pickup was parked and Tom Rabe could be found. After a mile of slow walking, he found Tom and Jerome drinking water and resting alongside the pickup.

"Welcome back, stranger," teased Tom. "We thought you had decided to take the entire afternoon off. Forget it; no chance you can do that. We're heading back to Reservoir Hill where those weeds are still waiting for you. Maybe you can start a fire and burn them off," he said with a chuckle.

"Tom, if it's just the same to you, I'd rather use my shovel to fight weeds. I've had enough work with burlap bags and fighting fire for one day," answered Scott smiling. He laid his shovel in the back of the pickup, climbed in, and they were off.

Scott had survived his first forest fire; gained some respect from local businessmen, and also learned a healthy respect for the danger of fires and how helpless a fighter could become when lost in the cloud of dense smoke.

Soon the summer was over and it was time to start football practice. He would need no conditioning for getting into shape. His legs were strong from thirty miles of walking a day through the rugged Wyoming outback, his arm muscles from ditch digging were already as hard as rock, and he had learned there were better pursuits than being a firefighter.

Now, Scott had his sights on become a letterman as a sophomore, and making the starting football team.

7

FOOTBALL LETTER

"Scott"

No answer.

"Scott", she said it louder.

No answer.

His mother opened the door wider so he'd hear the noise from the radio in the front room and slowly wake up. It was too bad—his sudden illness at this of all times. She knew how important playing in the football game this afternoon was to Scott, and his chances looked slim. Now that he was a sophomore and in his second year on the football team, it had become important for him to earn his letter. He spent all last year on the third team and never did get into a game or even on the travelling squad. Today was the last game of the season and he needed to get into the game, if only for one play, to earn his letter and wear a big "E" on his orange and black letterman's jacket. Today's game was the traditional Armistice Day game with their arch rival, Hot Springs, and that made it doubly important.

Last year he had managed to make the third team despite having to miss the first half-hour of football practice because it conflicted with the Latin class she insisted he take. Reuben, Jerome and he were the only boys taking Latin, probably because they were altar boys—was that fair? He gave her a moment to consider his complaint.

"Is that fair?" he pleaded. "Just because we are altar boys we have to take some stupid dead language and are dumped onto the football bench! I'll never make it into a game and earn a letter."

Latin conflicted with the first half hour of football practice and he could not leave classes early with the other football guys, so he'd have to show up late and miss the warm-up. Boys who took Latin seldom became football stars; as a consequence, he hated Latin. With a lot of hustle, he still managed to get suited up late for practice and pull on his jockey strap, shoulder pads, rib pads, hip pads, thigh pads, football cleats, a helmet, and make the 3rd team. That was last year when he was a freshman, but almost no freshman ever earned a letter anyway; so, he was not overly disappointed but even at that he still hated Latin.

Now this year he was a sophomore and taking Latin Two, so it was the same deal. He occasionally made the 2nd team for a scrimmage even with the late start and had made the traveling squad for away games, but was yet to get into a game for even the single play required to earn a letter. He had argued with his parents about taking Latin.

"Why do I have to take a dead language," he asked? "There are only three boys in Latin class with all the girls, and all of us are altar boys, which is why we have to take Latin—that doesn't seem fair. The reason the teacher, Miss Uhl, learned Latin even though she is Methodist is because when she was in high school it was a required subject for everyone so they could learn the roots of their English language. Learn the roots—what does that mean? Nothing! Roma in Italia Est," he chanted in a momentary lull as his mother stood in silence. "Anyway, I hate Latin. When all the other guys are going to football practice, I'm held hostage to learn roots. Mea culpa, mea culpa, mea maxima culpa."

Now his chances seemed doomed. Last night he came down with something—vomiting three times. It might be only caused by the excitement, but could also be something more serious like a touch of the stomach virus—although there could be nothing more serious to Scott than getting into that game. His mother would try one more time.

"Scott."

He slowly emerged from the fog of a sound sleep and opened his eyes. "Yeah, Mother," He murmured.

"How are you feeling this morning?"

"I feel fine," he said with as much gusto as he could muster when he remembered about the football game. "Okay? Can I get up now?"

"Not yet, Scott. Let me take your temperature. Here put this thermometer in your mouth under your tongue."

"I feel fine. My stomach's okay now. Mother, I don't have a temperature, I swear it. My God, it's ten O'clock!" he hollered as he looked at the alarm clock. "Time to get up and start the pregame routine like the coach told us to do. I've got to get something in my stomach. Mother, you know the pre-game routine, poached eggs and toast," he directed, as if she had not been schooled in the procedure by him a dozen times.

"Yes, Scott, I know the routine, but first we have to see if you have a temperature or have a virus and have to stay in bed." How very well she knew that pregame routine. It had started with his older brothers who did it religiously before every game, but Edwin did not get into a game until his junior year. When he finally earned his letter—it was a "B" at their high school in Buffalo Gap—it was probably the greatest day in his life. Scott is already a better athlete and might make it in his sophomore year in this new school, but the odds were against it. New kids in Edgemont seldom earned a football letter until their junior or senior year.

"Okay, Scott, your temperature seems much improved. I suspect you had some sort of a one-day bug that came quickly and has passed, so you can get up and I'll prepare your training breakfast," she announced along with a caution. "You'd better eat lite, and then hurry the process so you can get to school in time for the pregame warm-ups."

He jumped out of bed too fast, suddenly became dizzy, and grabbed a bedpost so his mother would not notice. Then slowly everything became steady and he felt okay; certainly well enough to suit up with the team. It was the last game of the season and his last chance to earn a letter. He was a halfback on the third team and prepared to play the assigned positions on both offense and defense. On offense he would be a running halfback and on defense would be a defensive corner back.

According to high school football rules, everyone had to play both ways on offense and defense because once they were substituted and pulled from the game they could not return during that same half. That was to avoid specialist and insure they were all-around athletes. As a consequence there were few substitutions and only starters on the first team usually played in the game. Guys on the second team were seldom used for substitution unless for an injury. Guys like Scott on the third team spent the games walking up and down the sidelines one step behind, and shadowing the coach. Today was the last game of the year and his only chance to earn a letter by getting into the game for at least one play—hardly a chance at all.

After breakfast, his dad drove him to the dressing rooms in the Armory and he jumped out of the car and rushed down stairs to the locker room. Coach Jackley was standing by the door.

"Scott, I'm surprised to see you," he said amazed. "Your Dad told me last night that you were sick in bed and would probably miss the game today."

"Naugh, Coach, it was just a little bug and now it's all gone," he said with confidence. "I'm ready to play in the game today."

"Good, we might need you because Daum has a bad leg and Art Pearce is limping, so get a good warm up in case we need to put you in."

Art Pearce was in front of his locker adjusting his helmet. He was a good friend, but secretly Scott hoped his limp had not improved.

"Scott, what are you doing here? The coach told me you were sick and home in bed."

"Naugh! I had a little bug last night, but I'm fine today," he responded with as strong a voice as he could muster; although, his stomach was already beginning to feel squeamish again. "Coach told me you were limping today from that hit you got last week in scrimmage."

"Naugh, I'm fine," responded Pearce. "Just a little sore, but I'm ready to play the right halfback position if Daum gets hurt. Well I'm heading out. See you on the field."

If Daum got hurt; Pearce said he was okay? Fat chance that left for Scott! Well, there went his chances for getting into the game—and last chance to get a football letter.

The entire team ran as a group from the dressing rooming in the basement of the National Guard Armory past the parked cars and the crowd of fans standing on the sidelines and onto the field where the team was met with a roar from the pep section and the Edgemont crowd. Edgemont had a long tradition as a football town with strong support from the local folks, and most the men in town had been on the team in prior years when they were in high school. Since the school had no bleachers, the crowd lined the sidelines intermixed with the players, and walked up and down with the play of the game. Edgemont crowd stood on one side and Hot Springs people across the way. A bigger than normal throng came today since this was the traditional last game for the year—Hot Springs was their arch rival—and if Edgemont won this one, it would make a winning record for the season. This game meant everything.

The team took their places for the warm-up and stood spread across the field in four lines with the captain, Sheldon Wade, out in front facing the team and leading the exercises. The long line in the first row consisted of the eleven men on the starting team. In the second row was the substitute second team. Behind them in a third row were the players who would warm the bench—figuratively, since there was no bench. Finally in the back row all by themselves stood Scott with Jerome to take their warm-up exercises. They did not get to always travel on the team bus to away games, but could suit up and join with the team for home games.

The cheer leaders were leading the pep club in one cheer after the other. Scott saw Kelly standing in the pep section. He dare not wave, even thought he was sweet on her. She was wearing the Edgemont pep sweater, and looked great. Like all the rest of the cheering section Kelly seemed to be giving her attention to the team starters in the first row and had eyes only for them.

Then Scott saw his dad and mother standing among the crowd at the ten yard line with his little brother and sister alongside. They waved to him, but he was doing the jumping jacks and could not wave back—it was not considered cool, anyway, for a member of the team to acknowledge people along the sidelines. It was an unwritten rule that the team ignores the crowd on the sidelines, and it was easy for him to do because no one except for his parents was even looking in his direction. It was kind of embarrassing to be exercising in the last row where everyone knew you were on the absolute bottom rung of the team.

Then the jumping jacks were completed and everyone except for the eleven starting players ran to the sidelines at the fifty yard marker where they stood alongside each other behind the coach, looking across the field at the Hot Springs players who stood alongside their coach.

"Boy! Those Hot Springs guys look mighty big," observed Jerome to Scott who was standing at his side. "They must have fifty guys over there, twice as many as us."

"Naugh, they're not so big and tough, it's just those blue and white uniforms that make them seem bigger," responded Scott. He moved up the sidelines in the direction where Coach Jackley was standing so he might get in his line of sight. He wanted to be standing close to him in case he was needed.

In fact, those Hot Springs players did look big and mighty tough to Scott in their blue and white uniforms, and they must really be rough because they had lost only two games this year while winning six. That was two more than Edgemont had won. Today would be a difficult game to win.

After the beginning kickoff, Scott stood on the sidelines trying to keep a forced smile on his face. It was hard for him to do.

"Scott, do you think we'll get to go in?" queried Jerome, knowing what the response would be; Hot Springs was ahead and neither of them would get in the game.

Scott grimaced. "We've got a chance," he replied, ever the optimist.

The first half ended and the team ran back to the dressing room in the Armory. The coach gathered them together and gave his pet talk:

"Boys, this is your last game of the year, and for some of you the last game of your high school career. This is not a practice session or a dress rehearsal; it is the real thing. It is when men are separated from boys. Now I want you to go back onto that field, and fight; perform like you have never done before," he exclaimed sharply and then paused a minute for emphasis.

"Execute! Damn it! Execute like you've learned in practice. We can beat these guys. Yes, we can! Yes we can! We can beat Hot Springs! Now let's go out there and get the job done!"

The team roared "Yes we can, yes we can" in affirmation as they rushed from the room and took the stairs going up two-at-a-time.

It was now almost the end of the fourth quarter and the game nearly over with only minutes to play. Edgemont was down by three points and it looked bleak. Daum, the first string halfback, had been tackled hard and the coach pulled him out of the game because of his bad leg. The other halfback, Art Pearce, was moved over to the other halfback position and made a good run and carried the ball to the Hot Springs ten yard line, but suddenly Pearce was down on his back and injured. The game was nearly over with only seconds left, but time was called and the clock stopped due to the injury.

Coach Jackley ran onto the field and knelt down over Pearce who lay on his back. The coach held smelling salts under his nose, the usual procedure to revive someone down; but Pearce continued lying on his back. Then the coach slowly helped him to his feet and with the assistance of the right end, Claphan, and the quarterback, Wade, they carried him to the sideline.

"Scott, go in for Pearce," yelled Coach Jackley, "and be sure to report to the official."

Scott rushed onto the field and joined the huddle. The quarterback, Wade, was already giving the next play.

"Okay, we need ten yards for a touchdown and it's the last chance we've got. Time is running out. They will be expecting a run to the right because we've done it all game. They expect us to run right. They won't be expecting a substitute to get the call and run to the left; so, Scott, we'll run you to the weak side around the left end. The play is number 26, and Scott, you've got to move out fast and follow Claphan around the left end. Claphan, you've got to take out their end or the play is dead. This will be a trick count. Listen closely. Instead of starting on two, we will start on the third hik and try to pull them offside. Remember, it's the third hik, not the second. Let's go!"

Scott ran to his position as halfback in the T formation, with Wade under the center to receive the ball. Scott was in the halfback squat position, like he had practiced a hundred times before. His heart was pounding wildly and mouth so dry he couldn't swallow. The quarterback was supposed to toss the ball to him as he headed left to the weak side while everyone else was moving right. Maybe it would fool the other team.

"Get set! Hik, Hik, Hik," bellowed the quarterback, and then a whistle blew. The Edgemont right tackle, Dawes, was offside. He had jumped on the second hik. The referee marked off the five yard penalty, so now the team had to make fifteen yards instead of the prior ten. This would be the final play—their only chance for a touchdown. The last play! Edgemont needed a huge fifteen yards for a touchdown and it was up to Scott to get it.

"Get set! Hik! Hik! Hik!" yelled Wade. The rest the team all ran to the right; Scott took off running to the left and the football came flying back. Catching it with both hands, he tucked it into his belly, cradling it tightly just like the coach taught. Claphan had moved out in front and it was his job to lead the way, block the tight end, and clear the way.

Scott ran as fast as his legs would carry him and Claphan hit the big guy on the end with a cross body block, taking him down and making an opening. Darting past them, Scott kept running down the field as fast as he could and was surprised after ten yards he was still on his feet and running. Then he saw the white line for the end zone getting closer.

Wham!! He flew through the air and hit the ground hard—very hard—landing on solid dirt. It hurt. Really hurt! The collision with the tackler was bad enough, he expected that, but the impact with the ground was even worse, it seemed made of rock. It was the hardest he'd ever been tackled, but this was a real game against the archrival, Hot Springs, and not just a practice scrimmage; but Scott held onto the ball—he did not fumble. Then as he lay on the ground writhing in pain he heard the cry: "TOUCHDOWN!!"

He lay there in too much pain to move, but team members pulled him to his feet, embracing him, slapping him on the helmet.

"Scott, great run," someone yelled. "You made it all the way to the end zone and a touchdown! "We won the game! My God—Scott, what a run!!" Slowly he stood, feeling woozy and weak on his feet, but all the team was holding him up and supporting him with their arms, and carrying him to sidelines where the cheerleaders were shouting his name. Everyone was rushing onto the field; Kelly ran across the field flinging her arms on his shoulders from behind and gave the back of his helmet a telling tap.

"Great game, Scott!" Kelly yelled. "You won the game for Edgemont. Hooray for you!" Even though he hurt all over, Scott suddenly felt good; he had gotten into the game and made the crucial last play—a winning touchdown.

Then as his mind cleared, it dawned on him that now he might even earn a letter and could wear the gold and black letterman's jacket. Wow! That would be great. Even though his hip still throbbed from that rough tackle, he felt good. It was a great day. He was only a sophomore, but now would be a letterman in Edgemont High School. On top of that, they even won the game. Life for him could never be better!

MOTHER AND DAD

Scott's Dad, Bernie Keating, learned banking mostly on-the-job. After being rejected from the draft because of a missing thumb during World War One, he briefly studied bookkeeping while working in gold mines in the Black Hills. One Friday morning the banker in Custer told him about a job opening at the bank in Belle Fourche. His dad made a sandwich and walked the sixty-five miles over the weekend and was waiting at the front door when the president of the bank arrived on Monday morning, and Bernard was hired on the spot; his first assignment was to sweep the front sidewalk before customers arrived.

Then Bernard began a long career working in banks in Camp Crook, Buffalo Gap, and now Edgemont. Camp Crook, where Scott was born, was located in one of the most isolated regions in the United States in the northwest corner of South Dakota a dozen miles from Montana and North Dakota. When the stock market crash occurred and the country fell into deep depression, the Camp Crook bank was closed and Bernard was out of a job. It was a desperate time for him with five children, a wife, and living in the most depressed and isolated area of the country. While taking a course in Rapid City in how to sell insurance, he ran into Art Dahl, who had been the bank examiner that made annual inspections of the books in Camp Crook, and over the years they had become friends with many mutual interests.

"Hello, Keating," Art said extending his hand in a greeting with his good friend from the Camp Crook bank. "What are you doing here in Rapid City?"

"Art, you might never guess. With the bank closed in Camp Crook and me out of a job, I'm learning how to sell insurance. There doesn't seem to be any future in banking with so many of them closing. My wife and five kids are back in Newell with her family until I am able to get on my feet on the ground again with some sort of income."

"Yeah Bernard, these are tough times for everyone in banking and everything else, I guess. The bank here in Rapid City is barely able to keep its doors open. At least, I still have my job as a bank examiner working for the State of South Dakota." Then Art Dahl paused. "Say, Bernard, a thought just occurred to me. The bank in Buffalo Gap is looking for someone to step in and run the place because the old man, Streeter, is eighty years of age and wants to step down. You'd be perfect for that job," he said smiling. "Why don't you hurry down to Buffalo Gap and contact Bill Schneider, the president of the bank, and tell him Art Dahl sent you down. I'll give you a recommendation for the job."

"Thank you, Art; I'll sure do that—go right down tomorrow. Did you say the name of the bank president was Bill Schneider?"

"Yeah, his name is Schneider and I know him well. He is a rancher out east of Buffalo Gap in the Harrison Flat area. I'm not sure exactly where his ranch is located, but Streeter should be able to help you. He's been failing in health and is anxious for the bank to get a replacement."

"Thank you, Art, and I'll look forward to see you coming to the Buffalo Gap Bank wearing your bank examiner hat."

"Good luck in Buffalo Gap," responded Art Dahl. "Goodbye, and say hello to Ethel," and they shook hands again.

From that brief encounter Bernard Keating began his new banking career in Buffalo Gap. It was a tough job. He took charge of the bank shortly after President Roosevelt had become United States President and declared a "bank holiday" that temporarily closed all banks nationwide to avoid a "run" by depositors to withdrawn all their savings. Virtually every rancher in the Buffalo Gap territory had mortgaged everything they owned with no income to meet payments. On top of the financial problems, a severe drought and plagues of grasshoppers had hit the plains states. These were desperate times everywhere in America.

The top priority for Keating in order to keep the bank's doors open was to work with the local people and ranchers to keep their heavily mortgaged properties out of default. During the daytime banking hours Bernard kept operating somewhat as a cheerleader for the local merchants, and every night and weekends he drove out in the country to meet with ranchers and determine how they could keep their head above water. Gradually things got better from year to year and by the late 1930s Keating was ready to move on to a bigger bank and new challenge. He helped organize the Buffalo Gap Bank into a branch of the larger Southern Hills Bank in Edgemont.

Now in Edgemont, he had hit the jackpot with a wartime boomtown, but that was not the case initially. When he arrived in 1937, Edgemont was still depressed like all the other towns in South Dakota. Because of unemployment, the WPA was one of the only things keeping food on the table for many families. It happened that one of his boyhood friends from his hometown of Custer was Representative Francis Case, now the chairman of the U.S. House of Representatives Appropriations Committee. The U.S. was looking for a location somewhere to build a new ammunition depot for the storage of bombs and explosives to fight the war that was looming on the horizon. Bernard suggested to Francis Case that the government look at the possibility of some place in the vicinity of Edgemont. That suggestion led to selecting a location seven miles south of Edgemont for the ammunition depot, and a wartime boom town was the result.

When she was a teenager in Newell during World War One, Scott's mother had been a cashier at the local department store to take the place of a brother when he was drafted for the Army. Inasmuch as she had learned accounting on the job, it was a natural development after marriage to help her husband at the bank when needed. She ran the Buffalo Gap bank by herself for a year after Bernard had started commuting to Edgemont. After the move to Edgemont, it became apparent the bank there was nearly overwhelmed with the boomtown prosperity, so she began to work there to again assist her husband.

The phone rang and Scott picked it up. "Hello," he said, but already knew it would be his mother calling from the bank to check on things at home.

"Scott, this is Mother. It's eight thirty and I wanted to be sure everything was going okay and Betty and Billy are ready to leave for school."

"Yes, Mother, they are all ready."

"Did they eat a good breakfast? What did they have?

"I don't know. I think they had the same thing they always have, a bowl of Cheerios's."

"Okay, Scott. Well you better head to school yourself, and don't forget to take that report on Longfellow you finished last night."

He responded in an exasperated voice, "Yes, Mother I won't forget. What do you think I am, a stupid moron?"

"No Scott, you are a bright young man, and Dad and I appreciate what you do at home. And thanks to you, the bank was nice and warm this morning when we got here to open up. Thank you and have a good day at school"

Since Igloo was a government wartime complex, it was decided by the ordnance depot to rely on the bank in Edgemont for their banking requirements rather than starting a new bank on the project. To fill the obvious need for banking out on the project, Bernard and Ethel spent one day every other week on the government reservation. As they travelled from bunker to bunker they set up a table in the center aisle among stacks of bombs to cash payroll checks.

That process became perhaps the most secure banking operation in the United States. It was located on a government reservation surrounded by a woven-wire fence patrolled by armed guards in jeeps. Alongside their banking table in each bomb bunker stood two soldiers in uniform with sidearm and holding shotguns at the ready. The commanding officer of the Back Hills Ordnance Depot was determined that there would be no bank robbery on the government project during his watch.

Scotts' parents banking day in Edgemont began early each morning at eight when they arrived at the bank to open the safe, distribute cash to drawers, and make ready by nine for the rush of customers who had already lined up outside the front door a half hour before opening time. The bank closed at noon on Saturday; then their family weekend celebration began. With good luck, they were able to put the family in the car and head to their cabin, *Ethel's Folly*, located at Blue Bell in the Custer State Park. It was a fifty mile drive and Scott was usually behind the wheel under the watchful eye of his father.

During summer their time at the cabin was a fishing weekend. Scott and Billy were experienced trout fishermen as a result of a lifetime of following in the footsteps of their father.

"Scott, you fish upstream east and Billy and I will fish west toward the swimming hole", proclaimed Scott's dad eager to begin his favorite weekend pastime. They each carried a bamboo fly rod and a fish creel hanging from their shoulder. "Billy and I will probably use the grasshoppers we catch for bait, but you might try using that royal coachman we bought in Custer.

"What about using that black nat fly I had luck with last month?" asked Scott.

"Sure you can try it again, but it's getting late in the summer when the more colorful coachman matches the bugs now in flight and might be the winning ticket. Boys, remember to count catches from time to time because the limit is 25 trout per day. Clean your fish and throw the entails up on the bank away from the creek."

"Okay Dad, I guess we meet back at the cabin?"

"Yes," he said, "and mother is expecting fresh trout for supper."

Following in the footsteps of his father, Scott was perhaps destined to become a banker inasmuch as he had worked in the banks in both Buffalo Gap and Edgemont; however, since he never rose above the job of janitor who started the early morning fires, swept floors, and shoveled sidewalks, it was a profession that never seemed to appeal to him. He opted for other things in life.

9

BOY SCOUTS

Edgemont's Boy Scout troop #27 was hiking into Red Canyon to see the cave hieroglyphics. Who knew when those carvings on a sandstone wall were created? Or by whom? Locals argued whether by early aborigines, or by Coronado and his Spanish expedition from Mexico up into the Black Hills. The guy who owned the property where the cave was located, Old Man Bell, charged admission to hike in to see them; but after a visit by the Grim Reaper last year when he left no will, the cave was now freely open to anybody with the interest to walk that far up into Red Canyon.

"Boy, those carvings look old," hollered Don Clark inside the cave as he looked at the back wall. "I'll bet they are older than Kit Carson."

"Kit Carson!" challenged Bert Jenson. "Hell, he wasn't much older than my granddad. They are many times older than that."

"What's so great about them?" inquired Don. "My little brother in the first grade can draw horses better than what I see up there." Pointing to the top of the cave, he asked," Are those things supposed to be pictures of animals, or what?"

"Yes, boys," responded Scoutmaster Weckworth, "They are very old carvings of animals and things. A professor from the University examined them a few years ago and said they were probably carved by aborigines— early Indians—long before there were any modern people living here." That pronouncement seemed to settle any further discussion.

"My God," shouted Bert, "they must be even older than old-man-Bell, and he told us he invented the telephone—telephone—telephone—telephone," as the echo from the walls of the cave gradually died. The scoutmaster laughed. Bell had not been popular with the local population when he was alive, because they resented having to pay a fee to see what was considered a part of local nature—owned by everyone.

A Spanish Expedition in the 1500's led by Coronado is known to have ventured into the Black Hills and used this southern route through Red Canyon that was a deep gorge extending several miles into the bowels of the mountains. Red sandstone cliffs rose on all sides, giving the canyon its historic name.

The scoutmaster had led the Boy Scout troop into the canyon on an overnight hike. The first destination was to this cave that held the hieroglyphics, and then they hiked further up into Red Canyon along a dirt trail that was made by the first stage coaches that travelled this way headed to Deadwood in the northern Black Hills.

"Scott, not so fast," yelled Scoutmaster Jim Weckworth who was bringing up the rear, "Some of the younger boys are having trouble keeping up lugging their heavy gear."

Scott brought the troop to a halt so they could get a breather. As Senior Patrol Leader, he led the hike at a slow pace because several young boys struggled carrying their food and camping equipment. It was too fast for some boys who brought everything tied to their back but the kitchen sink. The Army had developed sleeping bags for sleeping in the open, but no civilians had any, which necessitated carrying blankets and a tarp in the event of rain, plus frying pans, food, and a water bag tied by rope and hung over the back. Food consisted of bacon, pancake flour, potatoes, and cabbage; none of it required refrigeration.

It was growing dark when the troop reached a place where the trail became much steeper. Scoutmaster Weckworth and Scott conferred on a suitable site for their camp site, and decided on a grassy bench that rose above the small flowing stream. The scouts paired up and chose their individual locations. After collecting wood, each pair of boys started their own cooking fire and prepared an evening meal of bacon and pancakes.

Scott led the campfire ceremony that night that was started by all the boys standing, holding their right arm upright with the Scout Sign, and repeating the Scout Oath:

On my honor
I will do my best
To do my duty to God and my country.
To obey the Scout Law,
To help other people at all times.
To keep myself . . . .

Looking back later, Scott tried to remember the first time he had said the Scout Oath, perhaps it was on that scout overnight hike into Calico Canyon when they lived in Buffalo Gap. Dale Lovell was the scoutmaster and Scott's two older brothers were on the hike together with the Sandy boys, Ira Thurston, Russell Bledsoe, and the Thompson boys. It was his very first time camping overnight in the outdoors. He was a new tenderfoot, and thrilled to finally get to go on a scout hike with his older brothers.

"Scott!" his older brother yelled. "Don't hold the frying pan so close to the fire or you will burn the bacon. Raise it up six inches and use a fork to keep turning the bacon over," he instructed with more patience than Scott's lack of cooking ability warranted. He had a lot to learn about scouting.

While that seemed like a long time ago, it had been only three years, but was like ancient history because now they live in Edgemont and Buffalo Gap is a distant memory. After becoming a Tenderfoot Scout, he worked hard on merit badges to get to the rank of a Star Scout before moving away. By that time the scout troop had already dissolved because virtually no one was left in Buffalo Gap after the war started. Scoutmaster Dale Lovell had already moved away and was working in an aircraft factory in California.

The town of Edgemont had previously maintained a scout troop before they moved here, but it had died in the midst of the Great Depression, along with virtually everything else in town. That's when the town had almost no commerce except for the railroad and ranches. Inasmuch as Edgemont did not have an active scout troop, it was the end of Scott's dream to become an Eagle Scout; he was heartbroken. There may have been some good things about the move, but that was one of the worse.

But he had not counted on his Dad. He had been the chairman of the Scout Troop in Buffalo Gap, and had even been appointed to the executive board of the Black Hills Area Council, and in that position had supplied leadership to scouting in Western South Dakota: he felt passionate about Scouting. When the Boy Scout movement started at the national level in the 1920s, he was already a young man and too old to become an active scout, but that did not stop him from engaging with the things it stood for. He helped organize troop #24 in Buffalo Gap in the early 1930's. His oldest son, Denis, became an Eagle Scout and received his badge at a ceremony at Mount Rushmore. Edwin was a Life Scout, ready for the final sprint to become an Eagle Scout when the war started, the population moved away, and the scout troop was disbanded. That was the end of Edwin's dream.

After they moved to Edgemont, Scott's Dad felt his son needed scouting in his life and the town needed a scout troop; so, he contacted a few local businessmen and, using his clout as the town banker, he managed to start a new scout troop. A local merchant, Jim Weckworth, agreed to become Scoutmaster. Scott was the first member to join the reactivated troop, and before long they had a dozen guys attending meetings that were held in the basement of the National Guard Armory.

> ... To keep *myself physically strong,*
> *Mentally awake,*
> *And morally straight.*

Scott learned the 12 Scout Laws and what they challenged him to do: a scout is trustworthy, loyal, helpful, friendly, courteous, kind, obedient, cheerful, thrifty, brave, clean, and reverent. Those were attributes he believed in, and they should help keep him on the right track. He rapidly earned merit badges and was elected the Senior Patrol Leader, and led the troop in the Scout Oath at the beginning of their weekly meetings in the basement of the Armory. They had fun playing the game, *Capture the Flag*, in the rodeo grounds. Then he passed one more of the required merit badges and earned the rank of Life Scout and next would come Eagle Scout. But that would take maybe another year of hard work.

In Edgemont during the war years, there was little tradition of troop hikes or overnights. The focus of the community was on things patriotic. The troop put on uniforms and led the ceremonies at the cemetery on Memorial Day, but did little else outside of attending the weekly meetings and working individually on requirements. It was his mother who kept pushing him to work on merit badges.

One of the most important, difficult, and required merit badges was camping. Among other things, it required:

"A scout must have camped out fifty days and nights, sleeping under canvas, or under approved camp shelter, or in the open—including ten nights on hikes, during which ten nights he has set up or improvised his own shelter and cooked his own meal, and . . . ."

He had spent two summers at the Boy Scout camp in the northern Black Hills, but still fell short of the required number of nights. The requirement for the camping merit badge was defined as sleeping overnight somewhere out of town and eating a campfire meal. He had little opportunity to do that with the troop, so decided to do on his own. During the summer nights, he hiked a mile west of Edgemont into the prairie, spread out his blankets, slept in the open under the stars, and in the morning, started a small fire and cooked bacon and eggs. After doing it the required number of times, he got the scoutmaster to sign-off on completing the camping merit badge requirement.

Finally, he completed all the required number of merit badges and qualified for Eagle Scout, and then was recipient of a very special honor. Francis Case had by now been elected as a United States Senator and was one of the leaders in Congress. His home town was Custer, and Senator Case and Scott's Dad had been friends since childhood. Senator Case flew from Washington DC and drove to Edgemont to present Scott with his Eagle Scout Badge.

After the Eagle badge was handed by Senator Case to Scott's mother, she pinned it on his uniform pocket lapel, and it represented to him the culmination of a long, hard climb; it was worth the struggle. As his mother pinned the badge on his uniform and his dad stood at her side beaming, Scott realized the badge belonged almost as much to them as to him.

"Thanks, Mother and Dad. Whew! We finally made it."

10

D DAY: JUNE 6, 1944

"Has D Day started yet?" asked Scott's dad as he came into the kitchen where Scott was putting on a jacket and preparing to run to the bank to do his early morning janitorial work.

"Nope," Scott responded. It was the first question everyone in Edgemont asked each morning. "I guess those bombs have not yet reached their destination on the landing beaches—wherever those landing sites are." It was like a lottery pool with everyone in town guessing when it would start and where it would happen. People felt somewhere on the coast of France was the most likely place to start the Allied invasion of Europe. D Day was the top priority topic of conversation.

Everyone in Edgemont felt a personal connection to events of the war. Most families had an emblem hanging in the front window with silver stars representing one of their family members in the service or a gold star for one who had died in battle. Scott's family had two silver stars, one for Denis and one for Edwin. With two sons in the service they could personally relate to the all the battles as they happened: Iwo Jima, D Day, Battle of the Bulge, VE Day, dropping atom bombs on Hiroshima and Nagasaki, and the end of the war on VJ Day.

Memorial Day marks the end of the school year in Edgemont; Scott had just finished. One week later, D Day, the invasion of Europe began. It was the biggest battle of World War Two and indeed, of any modern war.

Everyone in America had been anticipating D Day for several years since Hitler's German Army had chased Allied Forces out of continental Europe in a major defeat. When would we ever go on the offensive and win Europe back? Nearly every family in Edgemont had a member in the Pacific fighting against the Japanese or in England preparing to invade the European continent. There had been little good news from any of the war fronts. The only offensive operation of any consequence the Allied Forces had managed to execute was an invasion of North Africa. Trying to make a successful landing in Europe on the shores held by Nazi German forces would be an entirely different ballgame that would require a massive battle force; the book had never been written about to undertake such a huge and dangerous invasion.

Then a week later: "Dad, when I got out of bed a few minutes ago and turned on the radio, I heard NBC announce that Allied Forces have landed on the beaches somewhere in France," reported Scott as he was putting on his coat and preparing to run to the bank to do his early morning janitorial work."

"You don't say!" His dad responded in amazement. "NBC reported that? Wow! I guess it means the battle for Europe has started: may God be with all those poor boys over there. I'll wake up your mother and tell her, she'll want to know right away. She has a couple nephews in England waiting to go ashore in Europe and she'll be worried sick."

A relatively unknown army man in the 1939s, Lt. Colonel Eisenhower, had been quickly promoted to Full General and had been named by President Roosevelt and Prime Minister Churchill as Supreme Commander of all the Allied Forces in Europe. The American and English forces were still bottled-up in England. It would be Eisenhower's job to prepare and launch the invasion of Europe. The anticipation for D Day was heavily promoted to help improve morale of the American population, which was beginning to sag as Germany's successes mounted.

The exact date and place for the invasion was a tightly held secret. Nevertheless, the workforce on the Igloo Ordnance Depot had witnessed events which seemed to be an obvious prelude to the battle of D Day. Starting some weeks earlier, everyone was working round-the-clock loading railroad cars stacked to the top with bombs and ammunition. Since the shipments were all headed to East Coast ports, it was obvious those bombs were destined to be dropped on Germany in support of the D Day invasion.

Then following D Day, the daily news about the battle came over the radio in sporadic bits and pieces. A sudden storm had complicated things; there was no air cover for the landing forces. The reports talked of several beaches on the Normandy peninsula in France that were landing sites with American forces landing on a couple of them and English forces on another one. The American troop landing at Omaha Beach was identified with heavy resistance, and a near disaster. It was hard to know what was going happening: was the beachhead a success or would our troops be driven back into the sea—a horrible, unthinkable catastrophe. For some weeks the battle lines seemed to vacillate back and forth in a stalemate. Then casualty reports arrived.

"Hello, this is Scott. Who is calling," he intoned casually into the phone.

"Scott, let me talk to your mother," a lady blurted out between sobs. Scott knew it was long distance and thought it sounded like Aunt Bessie.

"Mother, there is a lady on the phone", he shouted to his mother as he covered the mouthpiece. "I think it is Aunt Bessie, and she is crying so hard she can hardly talk." His mother rushed in from the kitchen and grabbed the phone.

"Hello, this is Ethel. Is that you Bessie? What is wrong?"

"Oh Ethel," she sobbed. "Horrible news! I just got a telegram from the War Department saying Marvin is missing-in-action. It just arrived and I am beside myself with grief. What does it mean? What can we do? Nothing!" Then Bessie again broke into weeping followed by a long wail. "Oh God! Oh God! My son! My first born—gone. Just like that—in the short time it takes to read one line on a telegram. Oh God! Dear God!" She paused long enough to catch her breath. "What can we do? Nothing!"

Scott stood behind his mother and listened. He could sense the agony on the other end of that phone call. Marvin, his cousin, was Bessie's son who lived in Newell. He was the oldest and his favorite of all the cousins and considered the leader of all the grandchildren in the family tree. Now, it seemed, he was gone, a casualty of war.

Every family in Edgemont who had a member in the Armed Forces, and that included almost every family in town, dreaded receiving one of those telegrams from the War Department. Maybe someday the telegrapher at the Depot would type Scott's own family's name on a telegram to announce some calamity about Denis or Edwin. Tears came to his eyes just thinking about it.

The news from France was difficult to interpret: were we winning or losing? During the next several weeks the most gigantic transport operation in history was undertaken:

By June 11th, after only 5 days   –   325,000 troops were ashore & 54,000 vehicles

By June 30th, after 24 days   –   850,000 troops were ashore & 148,000 vehicles

By July 4th:   one million men were ashore in France.

Finally in August, after nearly two months of fierce fighting, Allied Forces managed a breakthrough in the German lines. By September American tanks under the command of General Patton were fighting their way up the Loire Valley in France headed toward Paris.

Americans began to breathe easier, but as they were to learn six months later in December, the terrible battles were not yet over. The Germans launched a surprise counterattack in the densely forested Ardennes that bordered Belgium, France, and Luxembourg, and caught Allied forces completely off guard.

The phone rang and Scott rushed to pick it up. The telephone operator announced a long distance call.

"Hello," he said tentatively, anticipating it would be another call from Newell.

"Hello, Scott, is your mother there?" He recognized the voice of Aunt Bessie.

"Yes, she's out in back but I'll go get her. Wait just a minute, Aunt Bessie."

He called and his mother rushed in to pick up the phone.

"Bessie, what is it? God, I hope not more bad news. You've had more than your share already."

"No, not yet! I just called to let you know that Blanche's son, Vernon, is in Belgium in some army group fighting in the same exact area where that Battle of the Bulge is going on. Oh dear God! I hope he remains safe. I guess you heard that Blanche is ill with the flu and unable to get out of bed and her husband, Hal, is working in Pasco, Washington on some sort of secret government project."

Scott did not want to hear any more bad family news and walked out into the back yard to get some fresh air.

The Battle of the Bulge became the costliest battle in terms of casualties for the United States whose forces bore the blunt of the attack. It was, nevertheless, the battle that also severely depleted Germany's war-making resources; they were never again able to mount a serious effort; the war in Europe slowly drew to a close.

A month later in February during the dead of winter, Edwin came home on Furlough. Scott and the entire family drove to the depot when a blizzard was beginning to blow. As the evening train from Omaha rolled to a stop at the depot in the blinding snowstorm, Edwin stepped from the Pullman platform carrying his duffle bag and fell into the arms of his family. He looked resplendent in his navy blue jacket and wearing a bluejacket's cocked hat.

"Edwin, your hair is cut so short I can't see any," shouted Betty over the back of Billy who had rushed to grab Edwin by the shoulders. "What happened to all that long curly hair?"

"Oh it will be there again when I need it," he replied with a smile. "The first thing they gave me last year at the Farragut Idaho boot camp was a butch haircut, and the last thing I got before getting on the train this time at the Chicago electronic training school was another butch haircut. I'm going to a new station with a new job, so I need to give a good sailor impression."

"Where is it?" queried mother. "Where are you going?"

"I've been assigned in a terrible place to fight the rest of the war," he said with a smile. "I'll have to live in the Del Monte Hotel in Monterrey, California, where I will be teaching electronics at the radar school. It will be a tough and dangerous wartime job, but someone has to do it."

"Oh, Edwin," Mother virtually shouted. "That is such wonderful news."

"Yeah," responded Dad. "But tell me what the hell is radar?"

"Dad, if I told you very much about it, I would have to shoot you," and he smiled. "I can't say very much because it is still classified, but it is something the ships use to help navigate and locate enemy ships. There, that is as much as I can say. Anyway, it's good to be back in Edgemont and I can't wait to get a good night's sleep in my old bed." The family had him home for two weeks. When he left, they were happy he was not headed to the dangerous North Atlantic. Denis was still there on an antisubmarine aircraft carrier with the German U Boats that were sinking ships nearly every day.

After the Battle of the Bulge, the Allied Forces were engaged mostly in a mopping-up operation of defeated German troops during the spring months. On May 8th, 1945, the German High Command signed a document of unconditional surrender. The war in Europe was over.

However, the celebrations in America were muted; we still had major armies and naval forces in the Pacific fighting against the Japanese. The war in the Pacific continued to drag on. Many Americans remained in "harm's way" on the other side of the world.

People in Edgemont had a ringside seat in watching the caravan headed into harm's way. Troop trains with young men in uniform hanging from all the open windows passed through town nearly every day. The sidewalk leading to the depot was a favorite place for people to watch the troop trains passing through. Several hundred soldiers jumped from the doors and windows of the train even before it came to a rolling stop, and sprinted up the street looking for the nearest liquor store. They were rewarded with a dozen places within two blocks to purchase a bottle, and then rushed back to catch the train before it headed out—to God knows where. Early in the war, the troops were headed east toward Europe. After VE day when the war in Europe was over, the troop trains were all headed west carrying young men for the invasion of Japan.

For Scott, the war became even more threatening as the possibility of his being drafted into the army for the upcoming invasion of Japan loomed ahead of him. While the minimum age to be drafted was now at nineteen, it was announced by the government that it would soon be dropped to eighteen years of age. Scott would turn eighteen in the middle of his senior year and might be drafted before finishing high school. After discussion with his parents, he decided to carry a heavier load in school so he could graduate early in his senior year before being drafted.

The war in the Pacific then saw terrible battles in Iwo Jima, the Philippines, and Okinawa. Japanese kamikaze pilots were making suicide dives into American warships. It was anticipated that an upcoming invasion of Japan would require an army the size of the Normandy, France landing in Europe on D Day, and hundreds of thousands of Americans men may be lost in the invasion and ultimate defeat of Japan.

Suddenly on August 6, 1945, Scott heard the news on the radio as he was preparing to run to the bank for his janitorial work.

"NBC had just been told by informed sources that a previously unknown type of new bomb capable of wiping

out an entire city has just been exploded over Hiroshima,
a major city on the southern Island of Japan. More news
later as it becomes available."

Over the next few days it was revealed that this explosion was an atomic bomb, unlike anything seen before, and so devastating it could, unbelievably, wipe an entire city off the globe. Then three days later, a second atomic bomb was dropped on Nagasaki closer to Tokyo on the northern island of Japan and it also wiped away an entire Japanese city from the face of the earth. Only a week later after this second bombing, the Emperor of Japan decided to end the war and announced that Japan had surrendered.

"My God!" exclaimed Scott to his mother on hearing the news. "Thank God for the atomic bomb. It appears I can finish school in Edgemont and not die on a beach during the invasion of Japan."

"Yes," replied his mother shaking her head. "That is certainly good news for us, but think about all those thousands of poor innocent Japanese civilians who just evaporated in the bomb blast because of their wicked leaders. I wonder what all this will mean for the future? What is an atomic bomb?"

"Be darn if I know," responded Scott as he shook his head. "I studied atoms in chemistry and physics classes, but I can't imagine how such a bomb would work. But I don't really care as long as it has brought an early end to the war and I'm still alive as a result."

"Scott," his mother retorted. "Don't think only about yourself. We did not fight this war just to get a temporary peace, but to create a world without wars in the future. Think about it, if we can successfully build two atomic bombs then we can build a lot more of them and so can other nations in the future. Maybe they'll be stored in places just like Igloo, ready for use whenever or wherever. What then? What kind of world will that be?"

"I don't know," he replied. "What do you think?"

"I had two brothers, your uncles Claude and Clarence, who fought in the trenches of France in World War One. I had two sons who served in this war. Will it keep going on? Do I have to keep looking forward to having grandsons or granddaughters involved in other wars of the future, and on-and-on? When will it all end?"

"Who knows," Scott responded as he shook his head. "Maybe it will all end some day in a gigantic ball of flame with an atomic bomb confrontation."

She slowly shook her head. "Scott, that's a terrible thought."

Football practice began two weeks later in September on Labor Day. All thoughts of war were gone. As the team assembled on the field for their first practice, their lack of potential became apparent to Scott. Last year's team had won all but one game and had even beaten Hot Springs in the annual Armistice Day game, but the first string from last year were all gone except for Johnny Gallegos and Scott. They had no experienced players left, and not much of anyone else available to build on. The coach talked Bobby Nequette into coming out and join the team in order to have the necessary twenty-two on the squad for a practice scrimmage. Bobby was not even five foot and weighed less than one-hundred pounds; his shoulder pads fell down to his hip pads and his helmet nearly covered his eyes. He was hardly intimidating.

A couple other freshmen had more potential than Bobby. Scott's brother, Billy, was now a freshman and fighting for a position on the second team. He would make it, since there were only enough out for football to fill two teams. It would be a long and tough season for Scott; that was made painfully clear to him as the year progressed with one loss following another.

But some good can even come from losing; it became a valuable learning experience. After receiving all the acclaim in the previous year, Scott now learned humility and how to lose with dignity. He felt that lesson may have some benefit later in life, and it didn't take long for it to happen. He got a continuing taste of humility during those Saturday afternoon postmortems from Nate when getting a haircut down at the barber shop. He would have let his hair grow out long, except for threats from his dad that either he'd go to Nate's or his dad would start cutting his hair. Nothing could be worse than that; humility was truly a punishment, but he had to keep looking good for the girls at the school dance.

SCHOOL DANCE

Scott slowly hobbled up the entrance steps of the Armory where the school dance had already started, opened the door and heard the juke box music of Glenn Miller's *String of Pearls*. He was so stiff and sore from the afternoon's football game that he wasn't sure he could even dance.

"Scott, maybe you should forget the school dance tonight," his mother had cautioned. "Your sprained ankle is taped, but you don't want to re-injure it dancing. Sprained ankles are hard to cure." She gave him a moment to understand her concern.

"Naugh, Mother, I'm going to go." he said while still sitting down as he pulled on the blue dress shirt he wore for special occasions, reluctant to leave the protection of the chair and test his ankle. He reached over and grabbed for a pair of clean Levi's—his favorite—and pulled them up his legs while still sitting, then cautiously stood on his feet to lift them to the beltline.

"Tonight's dance is huge!" he announced. "It's—It's like a victory celebration—The best ever—We beat Hot Springs—And I made the winning touchdown! A team of mules could not keep me from the school dance tonight."

Scott also knew that Kelly would be there. He was hoping his fabulous run in the game might improve his status and give him an opening for the chat he wanted; he'd like to walk her home tonight from the dance. Kelly was a gorgeous girl with blue eyes, and sexy, particularly in the tight orange sweater she often wore to classes. All the guys seemed to think so, too, and were always trying to date her; but she had a reputation for being a bit moody—sometimes really friendly, and then other times not so much. The guys in the locker room talked about it.

"Well, Scott, it's up to you, but it's not as if you have the obligation of a date for the dance," responded his mother as she brought him a pair of shoes with leather soles for dancing. "Do you know of any special girls who will be at the dance?" she said with a knowing smile, having heard rumors from her daughter, that Scott was sweet on Kelly; but was so bashful he did not acknowledge it to others, and did not confess it to anyone. As his mother, she had always encouraged him to ask some girl for a date to escort her to the dance, or absent that, at least be sociable and invite the girls to dance with him. Last month when she and her husband were chaperones at a school dance, it became apparent that few boys danced. Most of the girls sat in chairs in a group as wallflowers, except for a couple popular girls or some with steady dates. There were a hundred students in Edgemont High School and only twenty in Scott's class. To his credit, at least, Scott danced with most of the girls in his class and was a good dancer. He had learned how previously in Buffalo Gap on the Saturday night dances in the Auditorium.

His mother dropped him off at the Armory to save strain on his taped ankle, and he limped slowly up the steps to the entry door. He could hear Glenn Miller music. Opening the door, he limped into the room.

"Scott," yelled Joe Daum as he rushed over. "Great game!" he said, slapping his teammate's shoulder. "I see you are limping, and for good reason. That was a great run!"

"Yeah, thanks," Scott grunted in mock disgust and returning Daum's gesture of a shoulder tap, "But we beat Hot Springs by only a single touchdown. Next year we'll have to hit 'em harder and increase the ante."

"Scott, great run!" said Bob Claphan who had been standing with his date had walked over and touched Scott with a shoulder tap.

"Thanks, Bob," Scott said in reply. "And thank you for the great block that helped get me around that guy on the end." Claphan was a senior and captain of the football team and considered the top athlete and most popular guy in the school; he seldom acknowledged the presence of a lowly sophomore. His compliment meant everything to Scott. "And Bob, we did it—we beat Hot Springs—yes we did!"

"Yeah, we sure did," said Claphan nodding. Then he returned to stand and talk with his date.

"Oh Scott, what a great game!" shouted Arlene Roselius rushing over from the opposite side of the room where she had been sitting. "You should be so proud of yourself," she said beaming and looking like she'd like to give him a hug, but constrained herself. Scott knew she was sweet on him, but he hadn't the slightest interest in her. For one thing, she was two inches taller than him, and was plump with big floppy breasts that were almost an embarrassment. He dreaded the occasions when girl's choice dances were announced, because Arlene always bounded over before any other girl had a chance and kidnapped him, pulling him onto the dance floor.

"Thank you, Arlene," he said with as much enthusiasm as he could muster. "Yeah, it was a good game and we beat Hot Springs. It never gets better than that."

Looking over Arlene's shoulder, he spotted Kelly across the room chatting with some girls. The music for the next song started, so he abandoned Arlene, walked across the room ignoring the other girls, and spoke directly to Kelly.

"Hello, Kelly," he said as casually as he could while attempting to constrain his excitement with the encounter. "It's great to see you tonight."

"Scott, hello," she replied as she slowly arose from the chair. "You made a good run this afternoon. Congratulations," she exclaimed. That was good, he thought, she mentioned the run.

"Thanks Kelly," he said as he saw Fred Guynn approaching to ask her for a dance. "I hear the music has started. Kelly, may I have the pleasure of this dance with you?"

"Oh yes, Scott, I'd love to dance with you." It seemed to him she had emphasized: "with you." He beamed and felt the blood rushing to his head and was flushed with excitement.

"Kelly, we may have to modify our dance steps a bit since I'm limping and my ankle is all taped up after the game this afternoon. You might even have to carry me off the dance floor," He hoped she would go along with the gag and followed with a brief chuckle.

"Scott, I think we can manage." She responded innocently, as if she did not know it was a joke.

"And Kelly," he hesitated for a moment as he considered exactly how to say it, but knew this was the time to make his big pitch. "You might have to help me walk home tonight from the dance with my bad leg. I'm looking for a volunteer."

"Scott, are you asking for a date to walk me home?" she said with a coy smile. "How dare you, the hero of the big game and asking me, only a lowly member of the cheering section, for a date?"

"Yeah, I've got a lot of nerve lowering myself like that. But gee whiz, I might not make it with my bum leg without your help. Anyway, Kelly, I'd like to walk you home."

"Okay, I'll save the last dance for you." He took that as a "yes." Taking her hand, they walked onto the dance floor. It was a slow romantic dance. With his left hand, he took hers and placed his right hand behind her back and pulled her closer. She placed her cheek against his and they danced cheek to cheek. It felt good, and things were going great.

It was a good school dance with the music coming out of Dick McKnight's phonograph player that he provided for the evening. They were too expensive for most families to afford, but Dick had the one his parents gave him for a birthday. It was one of the few available in Edgemont among the students and he also had a big collection of 78 speed records of hit songs. The atmosphere in the huge Armory was rather austere for a dance, but there were few other options where a school dance could be held. The Pines Night Club was a favored place for adults in town and the only location other than saloons that provided a place for dancing, but since it served alcoholic drinks with a back stairs leading down to the bar, it was not considered appropriate for school affairs. The large Armory basketball court was divided in half by a row of chairs placed along the midline roping off the north side and leaving the east side next to the stage as the dance floor; so, it seemed to provide a more intimate, dancing environment. Miss Uhl and the parent chaperones, the Parkers, sat on chairs in the corner. They tried to look as disinterested as possible, but all the students knew they saw everything going on—not that much of interest was happening.

Everyone who danced had learned to do it by osmosis; there had never been any instruction involved either in school or elsewhere. As a consequence, there were no sophisticated dance steps involved. The music was all in the rhythm of three-four time and the dance step a simple "two step", which involved taking two steps forward and then shuffling back one step. The only variation in the dance was a flourish on the one step back, together with an occasional twirl. It was permissible to dance cheek-to-cheek for slow songs, if the girl initiated the first move by lightly brushing her cheek against the guy's. Fast dances were mostly the same two-step move at a faster pace with occasional swing-outs led by the guy where the couple separated apart but kept holding hands.

A new dance called the "jitter bug" coming from back east was seen occasionally, but few in Edgemont danced it; it was considered by some parents to be rather decadent. Bobby Claphan and his date, Patty, had learned how to do it at the Pine's nightclub where it was a favorite with the inebriated crowd, and Bob and Patty occupied the center of the dance floor doing the jitter bug wildly. Other students didn't know if they enjoyed it or were just showing off. Scott wished he had the nerve to try it, but probably never would. Anyway, he did not like fast dancing, so usually fled to the sanctuary of the restroom when the first chords of a fast song sounded.

By the time the eleven o'clock witching hour approached, Scott had danced the obligatory dances with his classmates: Arlene, Wanda, Shirley, Ethel, Darla, and Shirley. Then he heard the familiar refrain from the recorder:

> "Sometimes I wonder why I spend the lonely nights
> Dreaming of a song."

It was Hogie Carmichael's *Stardust*, and the traditional song for the last dance. He rushed over to where Kelly stood and out-of-breath announced: "Kelly, here is what I've been waiting for all night—the last dance. I hope you've kept it for me?"

"Yes, silly, of course I have." They walked onto the dance floor and danced cheek to cheek with Scott mouthing the words of the song into her ear:

> "The melody haunts my reverie
> And I am once again with you . . ."

He though a school dance can never get any better than this.

They left the dance and as they walked down the sidewalk past the Congregational Church, his taped ankle began to ache. Maybe his mother was right about reinjuring it; dancing might have been the culprit.

"Kelly, sorry but we need to walk a little slower. The ankle I injured in the football game with that last tackle is beginning to give me a problem. I'm sure glad you are here with me," he said as he tightens his grip on her hand. "I don't think you will have to carry me; maybe just put an arm around me and hold me tight."

"Scott, you must be kidding me. I don't need any encouragement to hold you tighter." With that, she placed both arms around his neck, pulled him real close, and then pulled his head down to her and placed her lips against his in a long, wet kiss.

"There, does that help your ankle," she said releasing him. "If it doesn't do the job, then I've got more where that came from."

Whew! Scott had just been kissed by Kelly, and it felt like she meant it. Placing his right arm around her shoulder and holding her hand with his left, they walked together down the street.

"Tomorrow, Kelly, why don't we go bike riding and ride together around the town."

"Great, it sounds wonderful. Come by my house after lunch and we can take off on our bikes together."

As they approached her house, he saw a bright porch light shining alongside the front door and he contemplated how to kiss her goodnight when standing on display in front of the whole neighborhood. Taking his hand, she guided him under a tree in their front yard.

"We'll say goodnight here, Scott, so we don't have to perform on the front step with the whole street watching." With that she placed her arms around his neck and pulled him tightly to her in an embrace, and he could feel their entire bodies entwined from head to toes. She raised her lips to his, used her tongue to wet his lips, and then wiggled her tongue further inside his. It was unlike anything he had ever experienced before and his heart beat in triple time. He felt it from his head to his toes.

"Goodnight, Scott, I enjoyed being with you and thanks for walking me home." Then she unclasped him from her embrace, turned and walked to her front door, and entered the house without ever looking back.

The next day, Saturday, after lunch he rode his bike to Kelly's home where she was waiting for him astride her bike. It would be the first time he had ever gone bike riding with a girl and did not know the procedure for such a date. Not to worry; she led the way taking off at full speed past the Congregational Church toward the downtown and city park, and then up and down several more streets at full speed, with him following behind. He finally caught up.

"Whew! Kelly, you are some biker. I'm having trouble keeping up with my taped ankle. Maybe we should head back to the steps of the Congregational Church and take a breather. Okay?" He knew from locker room conversations among the guys that the steps of the Congregational Church were a favorite place of girls for necking, because they felt security there.

"Yeah," she replied, sounding a bit miffed, and headed her bike in that direction. She was waiting for him and sitting on the top step when he arrived. He hobbled up and sat down beside her.

"What a great day for a bike ride," he said by way of starting a conversation.

"Yeah", she replied without emotion.

He reached over and attempted to put his arm around her shoulder and draw her closer. After last night's kiss, he felt emboldened to make a display of affection. Reaching up with her hand, she removed his arm and deliberately replaced it to his side. Then without a single word, she walked down the steps, grabbed up her bike and rode away. That was the last he saw of her that afternoon.

What happened? He was dumbstruck. Had he said something wrong? Or did he do something he should not have done? No—they had hardly even talked since the bike ride began. He sat stunned, too confused to even head for home.

That night after supper, he cornered his sister in her room and described the afternoon to her. She was only a year younger and one grade in school behind him, and served as his confidante on matters involving girls.

"Scott, don't worry about it—that's Kelly. She's moody. Others tell me she's often like that with everyone; sometimes sweet as apple pie, then suddenly as cold as a cucumber. Scott, if you want my advice, get over it, and get over her, and do yourself a favor." Then she changed the tone of her voice. "Why don't you ever think about asking Penny for a date? She is my best friend, prettier than Kelly, has a great figure, and certainly nicer. I don't understand why you don't get interested in her?"

"You don't?" he responded in a puzzled manner. "I don't get interested in Penny because she is always going steady with some guy or other, and she goes steady only with guys that have a car and drive her everywhere."

"The reason she goes with those guys with a car is because they pick her up at the drug store and drive her home every night when she gets off work at ten o'clock," she retorted angrily. "She has to work every night at the drug store because she helps support her mother after her father got killed. Besides, those guys are also nice guys to drive her home, so there!"

"Well, I really like Penny and know she is your best friend, but I can't be at the drug store every night at ten o'clock to walk her home. She and I are good friends and always talk, but I never get any vibrations from her that she is interested in anything with me other than friendship—certainly not a romance. I'm not going to pursue her just to get turned down, and besides, I can't function getting to bed every night at eleven o'clock after walking her home. Can you imagine what our folks would say?"

"Well, Scott, give her a chance. Who knows, maybe she'd even like some dates with you instead of those late car rides home from the drug store with someone else. I know she likes you, why don't you give it a try?"

Some girls he could never understand, but at least his sister made sense. Forget Kelly?—that was easier said than done.

She was his first date and it ended in disaster. What about Penny? Was it worth the chance to ask her for a date sometime? She'd probably say "no". It was a risk he wasn't sure he was up to. Girls!

Forget girls; from now on, he'd stick to football.

HOMETOWN?

The pea pool game was finished with Bob Claphan the winner over Johnny Gallegos and Chub Bergen, and he won the fifty cents in the pot. Bob hung his cue stick in the rack and headed to Nate-the-Barber's shop in the plywood cubicle in the front of the pool hall.

"Talk to you guys on Monday," he announced over his shoulder as he left. "I've got to see Nate about a haircut; I've got me a heavy date tonight with a beauty queen from Igloo to go dancing at the Pine's night club. You guys take care and don't let any Hot Springs fullbacks run over you."

Chub sat down and joined Scott who had been sitting on a bench against the wall watching the game, while Johnny remained standing beside the pool table.

"Want to play another game, Chub?" asked Johnny with a pleading ring to his voice. "It's still early. We've got lots of time." He was right about that; they had lots of time—all the rest of the Saturday afternoon and it was raining outside with nothing to do, and nowhere else to go; and there wasn't anyone else they could watch playing pool in the empty parlor. They were football teammates: Johnny the right guard, Chub the right tackle, and Scott the quarterback. They were teammates on the field and buddies in the pool hall.

"Naugh, Johnny, you're too good for me today," responded Chub. Anyway, I've only got a quarter left and that is just enough to get a bag of popcorn and buy a ticket to the movie tonight: *Custer's Last Stand.*"

"*Custer's Last Stand*! Hell, Chub, don't you know he's the guy who ran around shooting at a bunch of crazy Sioux Indians like you. Why do you want to see that movie? I'll bet the Indian blood in you enjoys watching the Sioux Indians skewer Custer and a bunch of White guys.

"I want to see it because its history and Custer got what he deserved, the arrogant ass, and it will be nice to see all that happen again. Anyway, I'm only half Sioux Indian. My dad was White."

"What about you, Scott?" asked Johnny. Maybe just one game—no more than one. Please, just one?"

"Forget it," responded Scott instantly without even thinking. "You are too good for me today just like you always are, and besides I've got to be leaving shortly after the bank closes to sweep it out and do my Saturday janitor work."

Johnny walked dejectedly to hang up his cue stick in the rack on the wall and flopped down on the bench between Chub and Scott. They sat for some moments in silence, wondering what to do on a boring, rainy Saturday afternoon.

"Edgemont is a good hometown!" Chub suddenly blurted out.

"What in hell does that mean?" asked Johnny, puzzled by this sudden announcement of a nonsense topic for discussion.

"Just that what I said: Edgemont is a good hometown."

"You've got to be kidding," countered a confused Scott. "Compared to what, or where?"

"Well, for example, compared to the town of Pine Ridge on the Indian Reservation where I came from. Scott, you were there with me last year in the afternoon before the basketball game when we walked up the hill and visited my Grandmother. Pine Ridge is a stinking hell-hole where my Grandmother lives in a shack that's not much better than an outhouse. Lives there? That's a laugh. Who could live in a shit-hole like that? Pine Ridge is no place for me ever again: Edgemont is my hometown."

Chub was correct in his description of the town of Pine Ridge. Even though he and his father now lived in one-room apartment on the second floor above the Western Bar and his dad made a living dealing cards in the back room of the Western, it was a step-up from where they came from. Chub had no mother; she had long since disappeared.

"Okay, Chub, I'll give you that," agreed Scott as he shifted his position on the bench, uneasy with this topic of conversation. "Edgemont is definitely better than Pine Ridge, like a hundred silver dollars is better than a single paper dollar. I bet the reason you want to see Custer's Last Stand again, like Johnny said, so you can watch your Sioux Indians carve up a bunch of White guys." Then Scott led them all in a good chuckle.

"What about you, Johnny? Do you think Edgemont is a good hometown?" queried Chub. "Do you consider Edgemont to be a good hometown?"

"Hell! How would I know? I was born here; it's the only place I've ever lived. I've got nothing to compare it to."

"I'm an Indian and Indians have always been in Dakota," said Chub, "but you Mexicans came from way down south. How did your family ever get up here in White man's country from down in Mexico?"

"Well, it's a long story, but my dad came here during the 1922 National Railroad Strike when the railroad sent recruiters down to New Mexico to recruit Mexicans to come north to help crash through the picket lines and break the strike. My parents were starving in New Mexico, so it was an easy decision to make. That's when all the other Mexican families in Edgemont came here, too. They were hired for the railroad section crew because no one else would do that hard dangerous work for the peanut wages they were paid. Yeah, they call my father and all the rest of them scabs, but he had kids to feed—like me—and the rest of my family.

"Maybe you can explain something to me, Johnny. I've only lived here for a year or two," said Scott, "but it seems a lot of folks in town are divided into two hostile camps: the scabs, and all the others. Everyone talks about it. The Paul Kohler's are good friends of my parents and I heard Paul talking about it. He says since he was not a scab and would not cross any picket line and remained out during the strike when the scabs walked in, he lost all his seniority. All the scabs that walked through the picket lines now have more seniority than those who stayed out. As a result Paul is laid off every winter when work is scare. All the scabs, like his older brother John, walked through the picket lines and broke the strike, but kept their seniority and always have a paycheck." Scott paused to choose his next words carefully. "My God, that strike was twenty years ago, and it still divides the Edgemont railroad population into two hostile camps!"

"Yeah," responded Johnny. "The Paul and John Kohler families haven't spoken to each other in the twenty years since the strike. Everyone in town knows it. They both go to Catholic Mass every Sunday, but sit in different Pews; even their kids won't speak to each other in school.

Fortunately, none of them ever played on any Edgemont teams, so that never became a football issue.

Then the conversation went silent.

"Of course," Johnny said as an afterthought. "That was in the prewar days before hordes of transients like you and Chub invaded the town, so now all those former railroad enemies are only tilting at windmills."

"Very impressive, Johnny, sounds like you must have kept awake in Miss Uhl's literature class when we read Don Quixote," said Scott laughing.

"What about you, Scott?" asked Johnny. "You've lived here for a couple years and are the Captain of the Edgemont High School football team and your dad is the banker wearing a suit and tie to work and handling the entire town's money. Do you consider Edgemont your home town?"

"Hell, Johnny, I never gave it much thought," replied Scott after some hesitation. "I guess all of us live where our parents take us, or in Chub's case where his father brings him. We don't have much to say in the matter of where we live. We live where our fathers can get a job; it's no different with anyone. That's why Julius Caesar lived in Rome. You know Rome: Roma in Italia est." Then he paused in reflection. "I guess if you really came down to it, I think of Buffalo Gap as my hometown, even though there so few people still there I wouldn't want to live there anymore." Then he paused for a moment. "Yeah! I still think of Buffalo Gap as my hometown. Edgemont is just the place where I live." With the matter settled and nothing else to talk about, Scott got up from the bench to leave.

"Scott," said Chub, "maybe someday I can visit Buffalo Gap with you and see what in hell was so special about it. Anyway, in the meantime, I think you should agree with Johnny and me: Edgemont is a good hometown."

As Scott walked away he announced over his shoulder: "Okay, damn it! You assholes, have it your way: Edgemont is a good hometown!"

13

FREE THROW

"How're you doing, Quarterback, you're next. Climb up and relax; you don't have to call any plays or make great runs today," declared Nate as he motioned to Scott to climb into his barber chair. "You may be in charge on the football field, but I carry the ball here with my clippers. Scott, how do you want it done: same as last time with a little off the top and sides and a trim on the neck?" As Nate said this he tucked the collar inside to prevent hair from falling down the back and stood as Scott looked into the mirror, then swung the barber chair around so he could see the back of Scott's head, which was where he would start with his clippers.

"Yeah, Nate, the same." As soon as he responded, Scott wished he hadn't agreed even though Nate always gave the exact same haircut anyway regardless of what the customer said. Nate's haircuts were always too close and left no shagginess, unlike Bob Claphan's, that make him look more rugged than Scott, and the girls seemed to like it better—or least Bob always had a date. It was rumored that Bob's mother cut his hair—or only did a half-cut job.

Nate-the-barber was an avid supporter of the football team, although he seldom went to the games. Perhaps his loyalty had something to do with the fact that virtually every member of the team came here for haircuts. All their fathers and Coach Jackley went to Romanoff's barber shop across the street, the only other shop in town.

Another reason the team all went to Nate's was because the door at the back of the shop led directly into the pool hall. The barber shop was only a plywood cubicle on the front corner of the pool hall and either could be entered directly from the street. The pool hall was one of the few establishments open in the evening other than saloons, so the guys all gravitated there when they had free time on their hands, which was almost every evening after supper. They spent little time on homework; getting a big part of it done on-the-fly in study hall.

It was different with Scott. He did a lot of homework both at school during study hours and at home; when he didn't have any he'd read some book like the *Three Musketeers,* or *Tale of Two Cities,* or *How Green Was My Valley, or Silas Marner.* He liked to read novels. On Friday nights and Saturday afternoons, he might go to the pool hall but seldom played any games because the other guys were all pool sharks. He enjoyed just sitting on the bench and joining in the camaraderie. They'd try to sucker him into a game of pea pool, but it was a costly gambling game and he worked too hard earning his spending money to throw it away. He got up every morning and ran to his dad's establishment through the snow banks, started the fires, dusted the counters, emptied the ashtrays, swept the floors, and shoveled snow from the sidewalk; all this before breakfast and school. It would be insane to waste money on a gambling pool game he seldom won.

A basketball game often ensued in the garage on Saturday mornings between his brother, Billy who was three years younger, and himself.

"Scott, no fair," yelled Billy as his big brother dribbled the ball past him and raced to the basket that was an opened-up coffee can nailed to the wall of the garage. "Just because you are taller than me doesn't mean you get all the baskets. Anyway, that was charging and a foul!"

It was a close game being played with a small rubber ball in the garage in the dead of winter, the only place available on a Saturday morning with six inches of snow on the ground. The empty garage was available because with the steep entry way it was almost impossible to get the car into the tight fit. Scott knew that problem well—he pushed the end of the garage out two inches last week unable to stop fast enough after getting enough speed to make it up the slippery incline and over the two-by-four extending across the floor at the open door.

"Okay, we'll admit to a foul and you can take two free throws," Scott responded magnanimously. He knew he had to keep the game close or

Billy would lose interest and he'd be left with no one to play against. Saturday mornings were boring with no school and no basketball practice in the Armory. Maybe this afternoon he'd go downtown, get a haircut and even play a game or two of pool with his football teammates.

"You guys looked awfully good against Hot Springs," Nate stated emphatically as he swung the barber chair around to see the other side of Scott's head in the mirror, "and that twenty yard touchdown run you made was the most exciting thing I've ever seen in football." Scott was flattered, but doubted Nate had actually seen it, because he seldom went to games. That football game was ancient history over a month ago and now Scott was on the basketball team. It was his favorite sport. So far it had been a losing basketball season with three wins and four losses. Nate only talked about winning teams, so Scott would be spared a basketball post-mortem.

"Scott, that touchdown run you made to the weak side was a complete surprise. You really suckered Hot Springs with that call. Both teams rushed to the right where they thought your halfback was headed; instead you kept the ball and ran around the left end before they realized what was going on. You are fast and there was no catching you from behind," he gushed with a bravado tone in his voice. After a pause in conversation while Nate set the clippers down on the back counter and picked up scissors, he asked quizzically, "Tell me, Scott, when you are the quarterback and calling the plays, how do you decide what kind of play to call?"

Scott wasn't sure how to answer. "Well, I guess the coach and I talk it over before the game, then talk again during half time and decide what to do in different situations." It wasn't really that simple, but no need to explain it to Nate; he was only making barber shop conversation.

The basketball game next week was against Igloo and would be played in their Recreation Room out on the nearby U. S. Army Ordnance Depot. Like everything else in the Igloo community, it was located behind six foot fences patrolled by armed guards, and everyone had to wear a pass to get through the entry gate. For this special event, the team and all the Edgemont supporters were granted exceptions at the entry gate. Up and running for only three years, the Igloo High School had not yet established strong traditions and didn't even have a football team, but they started playing basketball from the first year when the school opened. Edgemont had never played the Igloo team before this year, so

Scott did not know how good or bad they were. He realized his Edgemont team was weak with little talent, and he was usually the high point scorer for the team, not because he was so good, but because everyone else on his team was so poor. They had a pathetic team!

When the day for the game came, Edgemont took two fully loaded buses, one for the team and the other for the cheering section and student body.

"Hello, let me see your documentation," announced the armed guard to the bus driver in an official sounding voice as he stood at the barrier across the entrance gate onto the project. Scott looked out the bus window and saw that the uniformed guard was none other than Paul Foss, formerly from Buffalo Gap. Paul had been owner and editor, following in the footsteps of his father before him, of the Buffalo Gap Gazette until it went out of business after the war broke out when the weekly paper lost all its customers. The Foss family was one of the only other Catholic families in town and their son, Felix, had been an altar boy with Scott. Paul Foss in his guard uniform and wearing a sidearm climbed aboard the bus looking and acting very official. Since the school bus's pass had been previously approved and no one required badges, his presence on it was only perfunctory.

"Hello, Scott", he said nodding as he walked down the aisle. "I hope you have a good game tonight. The Igloo coach, George Bain from Buffalo Gap, says they also have a fine team. Scott, good luck to you!" Then he exited the bus.

Some sort of joint dance and mixer for the two schools had been scheduled by Igloo for after the game. Scott led the Edgemont team onto the court in the Recreation Center for pregame warm-up and shooting baskets. The usual entry routine for the team was to follow Scott, team captain, who ran at full speed dribbling the ball twice around the hall with the team following, and then start to make layup shots one at a time on their designated basket.

As he led the team onto the floor and around the court, Scott was amazed to see the huge crowd; all the bleachers were full and people were standing along the sidelines. Playing their arch rival, Edgemont, was a huge event in Igloo—it was their game-of-the-year.

As they were taking turns shooting baskets and doing running lay-ups, Scott took a moment to look at the Igloo team. Then he saw Bill Bain on the Igloo team warming up. He was a classmate from Buffalo Gap, who was always Scott's competitor when playing basketball on the dirt field behind the school. Seeing Bain on the Igloo team was no surprise because his dad had been hired as the Igloo coach after the Buffalo Gap School closed. Although he and Bain were friendly and often played together since there were so few boys in town, they were never best friends—there was a competitive streak involved. They both insisted on being the top-dog.

At the mid-court line stood the Igloo coach George Bain, Bill Bain's father, who had been coach of teams in Buffalo Gap. Also sitting in a very prominent spot in front of the bleachers was Miss Ward, the school superintendent at Igloo, who had been in the same position in Buffalo Gap. My God, he thought to himself: I'm playing in front of half the population of Buffalo Gap.

Then between shooting baskets, his attention turned to the Igloo cheerleaders. Wow! My God! Who did he see? It was Meadowlark. She looked gorgeous—fabulous—in an Igloo cheerleader outfit with long hair that fell beneath her shoulders swinging wildly as she twirled during her routine. She was more beautiful than he even remembered. His heart skipped a beat.

Meadowlark was his first girlfriend in Buffalo Gap. They met when she was living in a teepee with her Sioux Indian family alongside Beaver Creek on the Sewright ranch where her father worked during summers. Her older brother, Swallow, became his best friend and Scott had even stayed with their family at their home on the Indian Reservation and attended school with them for several days riding a pony to school with Meadowlark. Wow! Here she is in her cheerleader dress and did she look stunning.

"Hey, Scott," she yelled and waved to him. He was embarrassed to be caught waving back because it wasn't cool for a player to be caught doing that out on the court during a game, but anyway, he smiled at her and gave a guarded wave back.

He and Bill Bain met at center court while shooting baskets. "Hello Bill," Scott said warmly. "I heard you were going to school here. You guys look to have a good team. What are Edgemont's chances against Igloo tonight—on a scale of zero to ten?"

"Hi, yeah well I wouldn't hazard a guess," Bain responded very matter-of-fact. "Everyone on the team is pretty new and we probably haven't jelled yet; so I give us about a seven."

"Okay, see you after the game at the mixer they have scheduled," Scott said, and the two continued shooting warm-up baskets on their opposite ends of the court.

The Edgemont cheering section was in the bleachers, and Penny and the other cheerleaders were on the floor down in front. Penny always looked cute in her orange and black cheerleader's uniform with the tight sweater that clung to her breasts and the short skirt that showed the thighs all the way up to her panties when she twirled. They were doing their routine involving pirouettes, and were close to where he was shooting, but she did not look in his direction, wave or acknowledge his presence. He was disappointed at being ignored by her, but hoped to get some dances during the mixer after the game.

The game started with a jump ball. Igloo had a tall guy, over six feet tall, and he easily sent the tip-off to an Igloo player. Bill Bain was a guard and Scott a forward, so they guarded each other when on a man-to-man defense. Bain was an excellent player and Scott and he knew every move of the other—they had played against each other for eight years all during grade school in Buffalo Gap. The game action was mostly between the two of them, inasmuch as they dominated conflict on the floor. At half time the teams were tied with twenty points each: Scott had made sixteen and Bain twelve. It seemed like a repeat of their games in the Buffalo Gap Grade School, which Scott usually won.

With less than a minute to go in the game, Scott looked to the scoreboard and saw they were behind by one point: thirty for Edgemont and thirty-one for Igloo. He realized as time was running out that his only hope was to charge at the basket and make a basket or in the process of shooting hope to draw a foul and get two free throws; so he dribbled slowly to the center of the court and suddenly in a burst of speed headed straight to the basket. Bain was between him and the basket so Scott moved as close as possible and shot underhanded in an attempt to draw a foul. It worked. Bain hit Scott's arm while he was in the act of shooting, and the referee blew the whistle. The shot missed the basket and time ran out so the game was over except for the two free throws Scott got to shoot.

The game victory now seemed assured with Scott at the foul line. If he made one free throw the game would go into overtime. If he made both of his free throws Edgemont would win the game.

Scott calmly walked to the free throw line as the crowd roared and the Recreation Center seemed to erupt. The Edgemont cheering section at the opposite end of the court was shouting his name. The Igloo cheering section was standing in bleachers behind the basket where he would be shooting his free throws; led by the cheerleaders, their cheer section was waving arms, banners, and handkerchiefs: anything in motion to distract Scott and make him miss.

The referee handed him the ball and Scott bounced it against the floor three times, his usual routine for shooting free throws, then he raised his eyes to look straight at the basket, and took his shot. The ball bounced off the backboard, rolled around the rim, and fell off the side to the floor. Scott could not believe he had missed. Now the only chance was to make his second free throw and move the game into overtime.

Suddenly the entire Recreation Center was silent. No one was talking and the Igloo cheering section behind the basket was motionless, holding their breath—utterly transfixed. This was their first ever chance to beat Edgemont.

Again the referee handed the ball to Scott who bounced it three times, raised his eyes to look straight at the basket, and took his shot. The ball hit the back side of the rim, bounced forward to the front of the rim, rolled once around the rim, and then fell to the floor. It was a miss.

Scott stood motionless in disbelief. He had made that shot hundreds of times, and now missed it two times in a row when it counted the most. He was devastated. Edgemont lost the game.

The Igloo crowd erupted in cheers! This was their defining moment. They had beaten Edgemont, the big dominating town seven miles to their north. They were a losing high school no longer: they had a winning team. The louder they cheered, the more disheartening for Scott. Slowly he started walking in the direction of the shower room.

Suddenly he felt a hand on his shoulder pulling him around. It was Meadowlark. Her eyes were filled with tears. Grabbing him around the waist, she pulled him to her in an embrace. "Oh Scott, I'm so sad." Then she whispered in his ear. "I was pulling for you even thought I had to pretend I wasn't. I've missed you so much."

"Meadowlark," he cried, "my little teepee girl. Gee, you look cute in your cheerleader dress. I've missed you, and missed riding ponies—and going to school with you—and staying with Swallow at your home on the reservation. What a surprise to see you here and cheerleading." Then changing his voice and in a mock scolding he said, "You were yelling against my team!" and then he smiled. "But anyway, I understand—I guess you have moved to Igloo?"

"Yes, the government ordered everyone off Cuny Table so they could turn it into a bombing range where the Air force could practice dropping bombs. After we had to move, my father got a job here at Igloo as a bomb handler. We live in a duplex and it's okay, but I miss Cuny Table. Swallow got drafted into the army and he is stationed in Texas."

"Meadowlark, after I shower and get dressed, I will be at the mixer. I hope you will save me a dance, or two, or three, or four."

"Sure thing, Scott, I'd love to see you and dance with you, but I'd better warn you in advance. Bill Bain and I are going steady now. You weren't around to ride ponies with me anymore, and I miss you. Anyway Bill will be at the mixer, too, so we'll both have a chance to visit with you. Goodbye, see you later." Then she turned and walked away.

Scott was devastated. Losing the game to Bill Bain, and now losing Meadowlark to him! What could be worse?

Scott walked slowly to join his teammates in the shower room. It was a long walk. The girl he always though was his girlfriend was now going steady with his arch-rival Bill Bain. He'd have to go to the school mixer anyway and put up a brave front. It would be a long night and a sad bus trip back home to Edgemont.

Next morning it was snowing when he got up early and ran through the snow storm to the bank to start the fires and do his usual janitorial work. He returned home and was sitting at the table eating cereal when his father was getting ready to leave for the bank and putting on his hat, coat, and overshoes.

"Scott," he said, "I heard from Betty you had a tough game last night."

"Yeah", Scott nodded, hoping that was all to be said.

"Well, Son, don't let it bother you too much," his father said casually while Scott continued to eat. "You will find in life that there are good days and also some tough one's that you have to take in stride. I hope today down at the bank will be another good day for me; but if it turns ugly, I'll work through it anyway and put on a good face. Thanks for starting the fires this morning down at the bank and shoveling the sidewalks. It's much appreciated and will make my day a little better. See you tonight."

Scott was beginning to feel better already.

14

CULTURE

"Miss Uhl, why do I have to memorize this stuff?" blurted Johnny Gallegos in frustration after he'd made a feeble attempt at the opening lines of John Greenleaf Whittier's *Snowbound*.

"Johnny, I don't actually require you to memorize any poem, I just want to encourage you to enjoy good literature," she replied in a conciliatory tone. "Look outside that window. It is certainly cold out there today with a covering of snow on the ground and feels dreary as we look at the gray shale banks beyond the barbed wire fence west of the school. I'll bet the sun hardly shines at all day. Whittier gave us beautiful language to describe this kind of day:

> *"The sun that brief December day*
> *Rose cheerless over hills of gray,*
> *And, darkly circled, gave at noon*
> *A sadder light than waning moon."*

"Johnny, that frames our day with meaning, other than just with a shrug and saying 'hey, it's cold out there.'"

> . . . *"Slow tracing down the thickening sky*
> *Its mute and ominous prophecy,*

A portent seeming less than threat,
It sank from sight before it set.'

"I'll bet you wore that homemade brown coat your mother made for you to school this morning and you were still a little cold."

... *"A chill no coat, however stout,*
Of homespun stuff could quite shut out,"

Scott decided to stay out of this conversation between Miss Uhl and Johnny, so he looked out the classroom window and knew it would be snowing soon and they'd need an extra bucket of coal from the shed. Hauling coal was the unpleasant chore he had every morning before school and again in the evening before dark, plus bringing in kindling and coal for the kitchen stove, and shaking the grates and hauling out the ashes to the garbage barrel. Those were chores of Dennis and Edwin before they went in the service, but now they were in the navy, so it fell to him.

"Now here is another reason why I encourage you to read good literature and attempt to memorize some of it," offered Miss Uhl. "It is one thing to listen passively to some dull radio show that doesn't tax your brain; but that mind inside your skull needs some exercise to develop properly—just like Johnny and Scott and Chub scrimmage to learn football for the big game." She paused for effect and stood up to walk around in front of her desk where she leaned her hind-end against the front of the desk in a rather unglamorous position; she knew this would get the full attention of the class. "Here is an example of good poetry by James Russel Lowell, from *The vision of Sir Launfal.*

"And what is so rare as a day in June?
Then, if ever, come perfect days;
Then Heaven tries earth if it be in tune,
And over it softly her warm ear lays."

She hesitated for a moment as if she was trying to recall the next line that involved a change of pace; then proceeded:

"Whether we look, or whether we listen,
We hear life murmur, or see it glisten;

Every clod feels a stir of might,
An instinct within it that reaches and towers,
And, groping blindly above it for light,
Climbs to a soul in grass and flowers."

"Climbs to a soul in grass and flowers?" She queried slowly as a question, and then waited a moment if someone had an answer. "That description is a wonderful way to describe the first blush of spring. Okay, maybe flowers do not have a soul, but nature surely does." Then she concluded with the finishing lines.

"The little bird sits at his door in the sun,
His breast the deluge of summer all oer'run'
"He sings to the wide world, and she to her nest,
In the nice ear of Nature which song is the best?"

"That is a fine example of robins singing in the outdoors during spring," she observed, "which is analogous in the human experience with a man telling tall tales to the throng down at the pool hall, while a mother sings a lullaby to her child."

Scott sat in the back row silently taking it all in. Johnny was one of his good friends and first string right guard on the football team. Johnny had a good head on his shoulders, but it was unlikely he'd ever be able to memorize much poetry. That was a losing cause. With charity in grading from teachers, he was a C student; however, some of the stuff about culture would rub-off on him. When the seniors decided to stage a stage play last fall, Johnny declined a speaking role, but did a good job painting a backdrop on the stage for an outdoor scene.

In the impoverished world in which he lived in a rail boxcar alongside the tracks that he shared with his father who was a section hand, Johnny Gallegos had already had his sights raised to a higher plateau as he gained an appreciation for culture from Miss Uhl's class. Scott knew this was true, because last week in Nate's pool hall, he had quoted Shakespeare to Bobby Claphan in a pea pool incident in which he caught Bobby in a questionable tactic.

"Bobby, to thine own self be true, then than can't be false to any man," Johnny mumbled with a knowing smile on his face.

"Are you accusing me of cheating?" responded Bobby.

"No, Bobby, 'Et too, Brutus', ergo Shakespeare," Johnny announced with a flourish of his pool cue, and Bobby began laughing so hard the game had to be temporarily halted.

"God, Johnny, don't start using that Shakespeare stuff on me or I'll forfeit the game."

Scott was rabbit hunting north of town late on a Saturday when he reached a bluff above the Edgemont cemetery and sat down. He was in the cemetery a week earlier to bury Jerome Colgan's grandfather who had died. The cemetery was a colorless and lonely place. The sun dipped below the horizon, dusk settled in, and Scott heard the Methodist Church bell ringing in the distance. The scene reminded him of the opening lines of Thomas Gray's poem he had memorized last week: *Elegy written in a Country Churchyard.*

> "The curfew tolls the knell of parting day,
> The lowing herd winds slowly o'er the lea
> The ploughman homeward plods his weary way,
> And leaves the world to darkness and to me.'
>
> "Now fades the glimm'ring landscape on the sight,
> And all the air a solemn stillness holds,"

That was as much as he could remember so pulled a tattered book from his pocket and slowly began to read the rest of the poem. Gazing at the headstones, he wondered about the people buried there in the ground. Certainly, none of them ever became famous beyond the confines of Edgemont, and most not even there. What meaning had their life?

> "Full many a flow'r is born to blush unseen,
> And waste its sweetness on the desert air."

The headstone epitaph that read (Orin Colgan 1850-1944) would be for old-man Colgan, Jerome's grandfather and also the father of Pat and Ed, current Edgemont mayor and postmaster. The eccentric old man had lived an obscure, drab country life in an unimportant town barely on the map. Outside his circle of family, who would miss him—perhaps not even them—or even acknowledge he was gone?

"One morn I miss'd him on the custom'd hill,
Along the heath and near his fav'rite tree;
. . . The next with dirges due in sad array
Slow thro' the church-way path we saw him borne."

The poem concluded:

. . . *"He gave to Mis'ry all he had, a tear,*
He gain'd from Heav'n ('twas all he wish'd) a friend."

Yes, he though, that would probably describe old man Colgan, and he sat reflecting on all those other unknown people under the headstones. He wondered if his own life would pass like every one of them: forgotten to eternity.

It was already too dark for rabbit hunting and maybe too late for supper. In the semidarkness he hurried along the dirt road across the Cheyenne River Bridge and on to home.

Even though he never thought much about death, he had to memorize the last stanza of William Cullen Bryant's poem, *Thanatopsis*, which had been a requirement for most adults in town when they were students. Scott's mother had to memorize the poem when she was in the Newell High School thirty years earlier. The title comes from a Greek word that means *death* and describes an endless caravan that trudges across the desert, and when someone dies, they join this caravan.

"So live, that when thy summons comes to join
The innumerable caravan which moves
To that mysterious realm where each shall take
His chamber in the silent halls of death,
Thou go not, like the quarry-slave at night,
Scourged by his dungeon; but, sustain'd and soothed
By an unfaltering trust, approach thy grave,
Like one who wraps the drapery of his couch
About him, and lies down to pleasant dreams."

All this poetry was making him melancholy, but next week he would play in the football game against their arch rival, Hot Springs. That would bring things back to reality. Nothing like a hard tackle to forget all about Shakespeare.

JUMPING HURDLES

"Okay boys, today is the start of the track season," announced Coach Jackley in the nearly empty team dressing room to Scott and Lloyd Putnam, who were the only two there. "More guys will be starting next week, so I'll leave you on your own to get in condition by jogging out and back to three mile hill." Then Coach Jackley returned to his office. In addition to coach of the high school football, basketball and track teams and a chemistry teacher, he was also the school superintendent and a very busy man.

Track started in March after football in the fall and the end of basketball during the winter. South Dakota was cold and students stayed indoors as much as possible, feeling cooped up, so Scott couldn't wait to get outdoors with the first sign of spring; track seemed like the start of a new year. Even before snow had melted, it was time for the track team to get outdoors, but the first couple weeks were optional and only Scott and Floyd Putnam showed up for practice. It dropped below freezing most nights and hovered barely warmer during the day. The weather was too cold for Coach Jackley to venture outside and stand around with only two guys who were only getting into condition anyway. His obvious solution was to meet in the team room briefly, give them marching orders, and then return to his warm office and a desk full of work.

"Well Lloyd, it's down to only you and me," announced Scott to Putnam in the empty dressing room. "The team seems a bit sparse, but maybe Claphan and Pearce will come out in a week or two. Anyway, let's run out to three mile hill and back like the coach said. It will be cold out there for the first hundred yards with patches of snow on the ground, but there is nothing like a run to three mile hill to get a guy warmed up."

"Yeah, it won't be so bad," responded Lloyd. "I'll be driving cattle this weekend at the ranch in a lot colder weather than this."

"Maybe so, but the horse should keep you warm."

"Are you kidding, I'm riding a saddle, not making love to a horse. Riding in a saddle and chasing cows is about as cold and uninteresting as things can get, but I have no choice. I have to help my dad with cattle on the weekends."

The Putnam ranch was huge and Lloyd and his father did most of the ranching by themselves with only one hired hand. His dad was the second generation on the place. Lloyd stayed in town during the week because it was too far to drive in from the ranch on the rough dirt road. Scott's dad was a good friend with Lloyd's dad, and they had been invited to hunt rabbits near a creek on the ranch. Scott always got several cottontails with his 22 rifle that made a good meal.

Track was a so-so sport in Edgemont and not as popular as football or basketball with students or with the local town population. Nate-the-Barber rarely mentioned it when cutting Scott's hair down at the barbershop. The track team seldom had a dozen members and few students or towns-people ever showed up to watch track meets. In fact, no meets were ever held in Edgemont and the team always went to Hot Springs to compete. The coach's instructions were simple: start with some stretching warm-ups and then jog out to three-mile hill and back.

A run to three-mile hill was a primeval experience; Scott often imagined he was a native Indian warrior going through a similar experience and fleeing an adversary on this rugged terrain the same as the aborigines who occupied this prairie landscape only a few decades before. Getting into the cadence of the jog, Scott felt exhilarated; he could jog forever. Their jogging territory west of the school to three-mile hill was barren.

Edgemont High School was located at the western edge of town and the sage brush prairie beyond was an isolated and forgotten part of the country. A barbed wire fence marked the end of the school yard and west beyond it the barren prairie stretched sixty miles all the way to the town of Lusk with nothing in between except for a few abandoned ranch buildings; the empty prairie gave new meaning to the term: wide open. Jack rabbits and coyotes roamed among the sage brush and antelopes grazed up to the school yard fence line. Antelope could often be seen by bored students gazing out the window of the second floor English room. The desolate landscape consisted of sage brush and cactus jumbled together with steep buttes, dry creek beds and was jutted with sharp ravines that cut though the inhospitable soil combination of gumbo and shale. The jogging route to three-mile hill gradually rose upward, passed over a ridge, and then flatted out with scattered sage brush and cactus.

Scott loved running through the wide open spaces. It became a challenge for him to push each step a little faster and hurdle over each sage brush with a little more flourish; ignore the cold air he breathed, sidestep the cactus with their pearly spears that penetrated shoes to the skin, avoid the icy snow patches, race the three miles non-stop, and take a brief breather at the turn-around point as he and Lloyd chatted; and then do the return run all the way back to the Armory, sprinting the last half-mile, and finishing with a hot shower.

"Whew, that was a good run," wheezed Lloyd as he stood at the summit of Three Mile Hill.

"Yeah," responded Scott. "I'll admit to being out-of-shape; that took something out of me."

"Let's breathe for a minute before we start back. Okay."

"Yeah, you've got a winner."

Scott's running mate, Lloyd, had run beside him stride for stride. They were good friends. Lloyd lived on a ranch in the remote cattle country twenty-five miles west of Edgemont across the Wyoming State Line, but during the school week he stayed in town with a relative. This terrain west of the Armory was little different from the rugged Wyoming country on his father's ranch where Lloyd rode his horse on weekends chasing cattle. He was a working cowboy who spent his time in the saddle. His dad's huge ranch extended for a dozen miles across the Wyoming State Line. Lloyd's participation on the track team was a rarity since few boys from the ranching territory were on Edgemont's athletic teams. For Lloyd it was motivated by the close friendship of the two boys with the support of their fathers, who were business associates; Scott talked Lloyd into coming out and joining him on the track team.

Bob Claphan and Art Pearce would come out later in a week or two but did not feel the need for any conditioning since they had been out for football and basketball and were already in good shape. They were less interested in working out anyway and more for competing in the track meets. Scott was also in good shape, but he always put in a little more effort to succeed at whatever he was doing than some of the other guys. Bob and Art were natural athletes and excelled without much effort or training. In prior years they had dominated local track meets each winning several events.

During the previous winter, Scott had been thinking about making a change this coming year in track. He was a fast runner and he loved the sprints: 100 and 220 yard dashes; however, he seldom came in first and was usually beaten by Bob Claphan and Art Pearce who were faster. Scott excelled in football and basketball because he did a better job of training and conditioning than either of them. In track he knew all the proper techniques for running a sprint, particularly how to get a fast start, but these other guys seemed to have more natural ability to run a faster sprint. Coming in second or third all the time in his freshman and sophomore years was not something he accepted lightly.

As Scott thought about it through the winter, he wondered if there was some other activity in track where he could excel. He observed that all the fastest runners had the same mindset as he: they loved the sprints and would not try anything else; so, the best runners were all competing against each other in the 100 yard and 220 yard dashes. On the other hand, the 200 yard low hurdles seldom attracted much interest during the track meet because none of the best high-status runners were involved. Because of that, Scott realized that if he switched to running hurdles and learned how to do it properly, perhaps his ability to run fast may earn some blue ribbons.

"Coach, I'm thinking this year of switching to hurdles from the sprints," Scott announced to Coach Jackley at their first practice. "I like the sprints, but I don't see any reason why I couldn't do pretty well at hurdling. Does that sound okay to you?"

"Sure, Scott, why not give them a shot; you've got plenty of speed and might do good in the 200 yard low hurdles. Let's work together and I'll help you all I can. Edgemont has never had a good hurdler before, so I won't have a lot of experience to share with you, but together we can work things out."

Edgemont High School did not have an actual running track with a cinder surface like most other schools; it was dirt. Located immediately north of the school was the Fall River County Fair Grounds where the annual rodeo and horse races were held on the Labor Day weekend at the start of the school year. A half-mile circular horse-racing track encircled the grounds and enclosed the rodeo grounds that were located in front of a covered grandstand. With the permission of the Fair Board, the school was given permission to utilize the horse race track for their team. While the dirt surface was unsuitable and covered with horse hoof scars after the fair if it was raining on fair day, it became smoother in the spring with the melting snow.

No one on the Edgemont track team in recent years had run the hurdles. Rummaging around in the basement of the Armory, Scott found some old hurdles that had been used in some prior year, and with the help of Lloyd carried them out to the horse race track and set them up. Lloyd helped him use a tape measure to get the exact specified distance between the eight required hurdles. Then he began trying to fun as fast as he could and jump over the hurdles in the process. It was a discouraging process. His times were not good and he failed to finish half the time because his foot got tangled up and he tripped over a hurdle and fell into the dirt. Apparently he had a lot to learn.

"Coach, I'm not doing so well in switching to the hurdles," Scott announced to the coach at the next practice session. "My times are not competitive and I don't know much about how to hurdle. It takes more than running fast, but there must be some things about getting over the hurdles that I don't have down. Before I give up on them, do you have any suggestions for how to go about it?"

"No, Scott, I don't because I've never had to coach anyone before in that kind of race. But let me look up some literature on the subject and I'll get back to you." With that brief encounter, he was soon flooded by the coach with articles on the subject. Surprisingly, one of the best was included in his monthly copy of the *Boy's Life Magazine* that was published by the Boy Scouts of America. It was good because it was a short article complete with pictures that concentrated on the three basics: (one) develop a consistent stride so you always had the exact same number of steps between each hurdle and with the same take-off point; (two) learn to 'step over' the hurdle, rather than jump and soar; and (three) push the leading leg down to the ground as quickly as possible while kicking the other leg forward.

The article stressed keeping feet on the ground and moving forward as fast as possible rather than soaring in the air, because speed is obtained with legs moving forward pushing backward against the ground and momentum is retarded during a soar. That is why it is important to get that leading leg over the top of the hurdle and pushed quickly down to the ground, and immediately kicking out with the other leg to gain momentum toward the next hurdle.

The article by-line was: "you may be fast in the sprints, but you will win in hurdles only when you know how to utilize the mechanics of getting quickly over the hurdle."

Then Scott went to work to perfect these basics. The first thing was to develop a consistent stride. The horse-racing track with its soft dirt that left foot imprints was perfect for that. He ran as fast as he could and then measured the length of his natural stride and compared it to the length between hurdles. Darn! It did not come out with a good answer and the distance between hurdles was not a multiple of his natural stride. It was too long for him to always take his jump from the same leg, and too short to alternate legs. Lloyd held a stop watch for Scott to run with shorter and longer strides and see which was faster.

"Scott, it seems to me you run faster and look more natural with the shorter stride," said Lloyd. "When you use the longer stride, it seems to require effort to reach out and does not look natural."

"Are you sure, Lloyd? Seems to me a longer stride will make for a faster time."

"Maybe, but Scott, the stop watch doesn't lie; it says the faster time is with the shorter stride, even though it requires one more step between hurdles."

"Okay, would you please time me again a couple times to make sure it gives the best time? Once I decide which way it is, I don't intend to change and will always keep doing it the exact same way with the same stride." The answer to use the shorter stride apparently allowed him to keep his legs moving for more push-ahead.

Then Scott went to work on mastering the jump: how to minimize 'soaring' and learning to 'step-over' the hurdle. He did this while also learning how to get his leading leg down to the track as quickly as possible and kicking out with the other foot to gain momentum going toward the next hurdle. It was easier said than done; it was a difficult maneuver and he had bruises on his shoulder from all the times he tripped on the hurdle and fell headlong into the dirt. But perfection does not come without practice. He was far from perfection, but slowly his times showed improvement.

Then the first track meet arrived with their arch-rival, Hot Springs and a third team from Igloo. As usual, Bob Claphan and Art Pearce won first and second in the sprint races: 100 and 220 yard dashes. The hurdles came next and Scott walked to the starting line and found three other hurdlers from Hot Springs and two from Igloo entered in the race. One of them was his elementary school playmate from Buffalo Gap, Bill Bain, who was now on the Igloo team. Apparently Bain had also switched to hurdles from the sprints since last year. They had been competitors from the time of the first grade and had raced against each other many times in the Buffalo Gap School. Scott was confident he could beat Bain in the hurdles, even though Bain's father was now the Igloo coach and had probably given Bill a lot of instruction. The race was neck-to-neck and Bain reached his chest out to the wire and won by a hair. It was not all that unexpected by Scott, and he knew he had work to do before the regional meet in April.

Just before the track meet began, the coach approached Scott and asked him to also join the half-mile relay team in which each of four runners would run a 220 dash and pass a baton to the next runner. Edgemont had only three sprint runners for this half-mile relay team: Claphan, Pearce, and Barkley, and they needed a fourth in order to enter. The coach approached Scott and asked him to volunteer as the fourth member of the team; otherwise without him they could not enter a team. Even though he no longer liked to run the 220 dash and considered himself the slowest of the four, he agreed to run the third leg, which is where the slowest runner is traditionally placed.

The 220 yard dash he'd have to run as a member of the relay team was just as fast as the 100 yard sprint, but it kept going at top speed for over twice as far, and Scott's breath was normally all gone long before the finish line. It was a mystery to him, but the 200 yard low hurdles was nearly as long a race, but he always managed to finish it with something left in his legs. Maybe it had something to do with the pacing he did from, one hurdle to the next.

The new half-mile relay team had never even practiced passing the baton before the meet and the team was entered at the last minute. There were only two other teams entered and surprisingly, Edgemont won first place, so Scott had at least one blue ribbon to go with his second-place red ribbon in the hurdles.

A few weeks later it was time for the regional track meet, which was the qualifying event for going to the state meet. Scott's work had paid off, and he won first place in the 200 low hurdles and easily beat Bill Bain by several strides. Then the half-mile relay team also won first place. So Scott had qualified in two events to go to the state track meet which was to be held that year at the South Dakota A & M College in Brookings. It was a first. Seldom before had Edgemont High School qualified anyone for the State Track Meet.

Coach Jackley drove his car to Brookings and carried the four guys of the track team who had qualified to the State Track Meet. It was a long all-day trip across the Missouri River to the eastern half of the state. They crossed the Missouri River on the bridge at Pierre, and then dove into the eastern part of the state, the trip a four hundred mile journey on a narrow two lane road. They stayed in a hotel and arose early the next morning and drove to the college campus where the completion was to be held. It was a new experience for all of them.

"Okay, you guys on the relay team all warm up same as usual," instructed Coach Jackley to the four members of his team. Since Scott was also a member of the relay team, he considered that meant him also, but it would have been nice for the coach to remember that Scott was also competing in hurdles.

Athletes were from all over the state of South Dakota and each wore his sweat shirt with the school name boldly emblazed on the front. Eric Johnson from Pierre who held the state record in the 100 yard dash was there with a dozen members of the Pierre team. He set a new state record last year and his appearance was intimidating with his huge thigh muscles. He was handsome, a winning runner, and he knew it and pranced around like he owned the competition. The Sioux Fall's team had at least twenty qualifiers.

Then it was time for the 880 half-mile relay race. A dozen teams were entered and all competed against each other in the final race. The track was a circular quarter mile track with four 220 yard legs; so, the first runner would run from the starting line and pass the baton to the second runner on the far side of the track. He would then pass the baton to the third runner who was standing at the near side starting line, and then that third runner would pass the baton to the fourth and final runner who stood ready to start on the far side of the track.

Art Pearce was the first runner, Raymond Barkley the second, Scott the third, and Bob Claphan, the fastest sprinter, would anchor the team as the fourth runner. The lanes were changed for each lap so that all teams would run the same total distance, so at the corners all the runners would be required to cross over into their new lane. Those who had started on the longer outside lane would now be on the shorter inside lane so everyone would run the same total distance. It could be rather confusing and dangerous when everyone was running at full speed and changing lanes.

Art Pearce would start the race at the starting line and as soon as the runners were off, all those running the third leg had to move onto the track in their new designated lanes. Scott moved onto the track and watched as Art Pearce ran his race and came in slightly ahead of some of the other teams, but it was difficult to see the far side of the track from where Scott stood waiting in his starting lane out on the track. Art passed the baton successfully without dropping it to Raymond Barkley. Scott watched as Barkley rounded the corner with the runners all bunched up and he could not tell where his team stood as they rounded the corner headed toward him, then Barkley reached out the baton with his left hand as Scott reached back with his right, already running near full speed and successfully got it in his hand.

Then he took off as fast as his legs would carry him running neck-and-neck with those alongside. The lane crossover at the corner went smoothly for Scott, but out of the corner of his eye he could see two runners colliding and falling down on the track. As he ran on the back side corner, he felt he had almost exhausted all his strength and his legs began to turn to rubber. He pushed a little harder and as he approached the line on the back side where Claphan stood waiting, he could see he was probably in second or third place. With his last ounce of strength he reached out the baton to Claphan who grabbed it and took off in a dead run.

Scott slowly walked off the track; he had done his best. Was it good enough? He watched as Claphan ran with amazing speed and pulled ahead into second place. Then the race was finished and the Edgemont Half-Mile relay team had finished in second place.

The four guys, still out of breath, all ran to the finish line and embraced. Coach Jackley was also there and joined in the celebration.

"You guys won second place—a silver medal—in the state track meet. Wow!" The coach gave each of them a slap on the shoulder. "These are the first medals an Edgemont team ever won at a state meet; wait until they hear about this back in Edgemont."

"Yeah," yelled Bob Claphan. "Wait until Nate-the-Barber hears about this. It might even mean a free haircut."

Scott knew his big race was still ahead of him, so he did his stretching and warm-up exercises for hurdling and went to the far side of the arena where some practice hurdles were set up. He ran a few for practice to get his timing down. It was a cinder track and easy to run on unlike the dirt track of Edgemont. There were too many hurlers for one race, so three preliminary heats were required with the first three winners from each making it into the finals. Scott was surprised to find that he won second in the first qualifying heat, so he had made it as one of a dozen runners in the finals. Then the final was scheduled next. As he walked onto the track and took his starting position, he looked at his competitors. They looked like they would be hard to beat. He got down in his starting position and the gun sounded, but the guy on his right jumped the gun and was warned that one more false start and he would be disqualified. Scott got down into his starting position again and the starting gun sounded.

He got off to a fast start and seemed to be running stride-for-stride with those immediately to his right and left. His pace was working out fine and he was able to take off from the correct position in front of each hurdle, kept his legs low barely above the top of the hurdles, pushed his leading leg down quickly after each hurdle, and kicked out with his other leg to regain the momentum he had lost when going over the hurdle. As he jumped over the last hurdle, he knew he was doing well and gave the final sprint all he had left to give. The runner two lanes to his right broke the tape slightly ahead of him. Some official caught him as he slowed to a stop and led him back to the finish line.

"Kid, come back to the finish line with me," instructed the official. "I think you finished in third place, but we'll wait until the judges confirm that." No one from the Edgemont team, including the coach, was there to greet him. They were off someplace celebrating their own victory.

Then it was announced he had come in third. Wow! He was the third best hurdler in the State of South Dakota: he was elated—more than he had even dreamed during that cold March day on the horse track in Edgemont. Then the realization dawned on Scott that he had even won two medals: a second place silver medal and a third place bronze medal. Wow! They were the first medals an Edgemont team ever won at a state meet, and now he had even won two—more than anyone else.

It was one of Scott's best days ever. It might even get some mention next time he got his haircut down at the barber shop by Nate-the-barber. That would be nice.

16

SUMMER JOBS

Scott returned from his morning janitorial work at the bank to a quiet house. Betty and Billy were still sleeping and his mother and father had left early for another day of work at the bank. After breakfast he picked up the *Saturday Evening Post* magazine to read a short story about a cowboy who was heading for a roundup where the rancher's beautiful daughter was waiting. He ran to the phone when it rang.

"Hello," he announced in a desultory manner, anticipating a call from Jerome who usually wanted to ramble about the upcoming day.

"Scott, Dad!"

"Yes, Dad, why are you calling?"

"Say Scott, a guy from a new Igloo contractor just opened an account here at the bank. They will be building sidewalks on the base in front of all the housing, and are in need of workers and will be hiring. It is the Long Construction Company and he is the manager named Jim Thompson. The temporary hiring office is just south of the Rec Center. I told him about you and Jerome and your work experience last summer with the city of Edgemont. He asked that you contact him and you'd have a job. Are you interested?"

"Yeah, Dad, that sounds Okay, and I'm sure Jerome would be interested to." Then he fell silent for a moment. "But Dad, what do we do for transportation out to Igloo?"

"Well, you can use our car to drive out to Igloo this afternoon to see Jim Thompson and get hired. Then I'll talk to Jerome's dad, Ed Colgan, and see if he'd agree to use their old 1928 Oldsmobile antique car for the commute. They never drive it anywhere. I'll talk to Ed."

"Okay, I'll give Jerome a call and we'll drive our car to Igloo this afternoon and get the job. Sound okay to you?"

"Yes, Scott, it sounds good." By that afternoon Scott and Jerome had a job building sidewalks at Igloo. It paid $1.05 per hour, over double what they had earned the previous summer digging ditch for the city of Edgemont. They were photographed, fingerprinted, and issued official badges that gave them entry to the Black Hills Ordnance Depot.

They found the job of building sidewalks was hard work and boring. A month later, after helping lay over a mile of sidewalk, they heard that a half-dozen of the Edgemont football team were also working at Igloo on another project as "skilled" roofers and making $1.25/hour. The need to change jobs for the higher pay was a no-brainer, but was prohibited by nation-wide wartime rules. They found a way to circumvent the rule. They quit the job of building sidewalks for the Long Construction Company at Igloo.

"Hello, Tom," Scott said in greeting his old boss, Tom Rabe, who he found standing alongside his pickup where two teenage boys were digging a ditch. Jerome and Scott had driven up in Jerome's old antique 1928 Oldsmobile.

"Hello, Scott, I though you and Jerome would be hard at work at Igloo this time of day."

"Well, Tom, that's what we want to talk to you about. You see, we want to get on a roofing crew at Igloo with all the other guys who were on the football team with us. The only problem is to get on that crew we need a new piece of paper signed by the last place we worked before we can be hired."

"Yeah, these damn government regulations. They drive a guy crazy."

"Well, Tom, you see," and Scott hesitated momentarily as he considered exactly how to make the pitch to Tom. "We've quit the job working on the sidewalk. It only paid one dollar and five cents an hour, while working on the roofing crew with a lot of overtime will pay us several times as much. Jerome and I will both need that extra money to help our parents finance college in another year. We were hoping that, Tom, you would sign a release paper so we can go back to work in the new job at Igloo." There, he had said it and wondered what the response would be.

"How much will the new roofing job pay," he asked.

"It will pay $1.25 per hour compared to $1.05 for the sidewalk job, but the big difference is the roofing crew is working 10 hours a day and 7 days a week, so we make a lot of overtime pay."

"Yeah that is a big difference," he said as he pushed back his hat in thought. "Well boys, you were always good workers for me; however, I don't want to get in trouble with the government Wage and Hour guys, so I can't sign it unless you actually work for me for a couple days.

"Tom, that is fine. Jerome and I will help your guys in digging this ditch for a day or two. Will you sign the papers then?"

"Yeah, that will be okay."

"Tom, we were hoping to not have to work for free. Do we still get our fifty cents an hour?" Tom Rabe broke out laughing.

"You two guys are a real case. Your parents did not raise any dummies or shrinking violets," Tom responded with a chuckle. "Sure, you will get your old pay again for two days. I will check with the Mayor, but since he is Jerome's uncle, I suspect he will give me his okay. Come back in the morning and see if you can still get a shovel into this Edgemont gumbo. You'd better bring some gloves. As you may remember, we're not like at Igloo; we actually do some work here."

So Tom Rabe agreed to hire them for a couple days working for the City of Edgemont. After working that job for two days, Tom gave them the necessary paperwork to take back to igloo and be hired by the contractor who was building roofs.

The job was nailing asphalt tiles onto a plywood slab suspended on stilts twenty-five feet in the air where bombs could be stacked underneath. It was in the double-fenced combat zone where all the bombs were stored in the concrete bunkers. The bunkers were now completely filled with bombs, so incoming would have to be placed on a concrete pad covered with the roof slab the guys were working on. It was a high priority job and the crew worked 10 hour days, seven days a week. It was hard work but there was a lot of camaraderie and fun working with the guys from the football team: Bobby Claphan, Art Pearce, Johnny Gallegos, Chub Bergen, Gene Parker, and Jerome Colgan. They got time-and-a-half over eight hours, double-time on Saturdays, and triple-time on Sunday. Scott was making $125 per week and by the end of summer he had earned nearly a thousand dollars. That would be big help when he went to college in another year.

Then in a familiar pattern, he worked again the following summer at Igloo, this time in special restricted areas behind double web wire fences sand blasting rusted bomb fins. The area was restricted not because of the bombs, but it was rumored that poison gases canisters were being stored in the magazine buildings.

During his senior year in school, with the encouragement of his parents, he had taken competitive nationwide exams to earn an NROTC scholarship at one of the many universities. There were only two Midshipmen to be appointed from the state of South Dakota. The terms of the scholarship were for the navy to pay the tuition at the university where he was assigned, and also buy books and be paid $50 per month. In return for this 4 year scholarship he would serve 3 years on active duty as an officer in the U.S. Navy. Inasmuch as every high school graduate faced having to be drafted for two years into the army as an enlisted person without the benefit of receiving a college education, becoming an officer in the navy was an attractive alternative. Scott passed the preliminary qualification and had to travel by train to Minneapolis for a physical examination and interview by naval officers. Then came the nervous time of waiting to hear if he had been selected and if so to what university he would be assigned for his college career.

He got the answer when he was attending the state track meet in his senior year in Sioux Falls. He as the only student from Edgemont who had qualified for the state track meet in hurdles, so he had to travel by auto with the Igloo coach and his son, Bill Bain. He had this other encounter with Bill, who informed him that he and Meadowlark were no longer going together. She had already been accepted for enrollment at Chadron College in Nebraska.

Scott was all by himself at the track meet. As he walked to the area where the hurdles were set up, he was surprised to see they were on a curved portion of the track going around a corner rather than on a straightway. It was the first time he ever experienced jumping hurdles on a curve, and found it necessary to take off over the hurdle from the inside edge of the lane in order to alight on the far side still in the same lane, otherwise be disqualified. In concentrating in an attempt to negotiate that maneuver, his foot got caught in a hurdle and he ended up flying onto the track. Both knees had painful scrapes full of cinders. That was the end of his high school track career. He was dejected: what an ending?

As he hobbled into the hotel with his bandaged knees to get his room key, the desk clerk said he had just received a telegram addressed to him. It was from his dad and he opened it to read:

"Scott, you have been appointed a Midshipman in the U.S. Navy and assigned to the University of Colorado. Congratulations."

Dad.

Hooray! He shouted in an empty hotel lobby. His college career was now assured with a scholarship. Nothing could be better than that—he even forgot about falling on the cinder track and his sore knees. Hooray!

THE PROM

"Oh Scott, Miss Uhl told me she wanted you and me to be on the committee for planning this year's prom," gushed Rosie after cornering Scott as he was taking off his coat and hanging it in his hall locker. "Oh Scott, I do hope you will agree to be on the committee with me. We'll have so much fun together. Okay, Scott, Okay? Will you? Please."

How could he possibly respond, like: 'no I do not want to be on the committee', or 'no, l do not want to be on the committee with you'? His only realistic choice was to agree—talk about an offer he couldn't refuse. In addition to class sponsor, Miss Uhl was teacher of two of his classes, American History and English, so it would unwise to alienate her. Rosie had been angling for weeks to get him to ask her for a date, something Scott had no interest in pursuing.

"Rosie, are you sure that's what Miss Uhl wants? he asked. "Wanda or Joe would be better choices for that kind of thing.

"Oh Scott, pershaw! You are the class president. We need the president on the committee to get things done." Yes, Scott was the class president but only because Rosie had waged a campaign to ensure that outcome. He was already captain of the football and basketball teams and another title meant only a lot of agony, like being on this committee for the prom. She continued in a pleading voice, "Scott, you will be so very great. I'll tell Miss Uhl you agree, okay?"

The prom would be coming up next month, but Scott was not looking forward to it. Rosie was overly enthusiastic because she was a social animal and things like school dances and proms were the center of her life. She was sometimes described as 'boy crazy'. Rosie came from a farm family twenty miles south of Edgemont near the remote town of Ardmore and was living with her sister in town to go to high school. Few guys ever asked her for a date. She was popular with all the girls in the class, but a pain in the rear as far as the guys were concerned: nobody could really be that 'happy' all the time.

Now with the prom coming up, it meant Scott would have to get a date, and that gave him the problem of whom to ask? He couldn't go stag to the prom—that would be unheard of, and besides, his parents would not allow such a social affront in the high school. He surely hoped he could come up with some girl other than Rosie, but who else to ask? He knew he would have to get a date because every guy in the junior and senior class was expected to attend, inasmuch as the classes were small. Even if all the guys showed up with dates or as stags, it would be barely enough to finance the Church Hall for a dinner, fill the dance programs of the girls, let alone have enough bodies to pack the dance floor. The social guidelines said a junior or senior guy could date a sophomore girl, but while it was allowed it was frowned upon; particularly by all the girls because there were so few of them and they did not want any competition from cute girls in the lower classes.

For Scott, a date with Penny was his preferred choice, but he realized that was probably not an option. He would like to take Penny, but she was always going steady with someone else, even though her boyfriends varied from one month to the next. He wondered why he didn't try harder and ask her for a date. Maybe in between one of her many romances he might slip in as her boyfriend. She was the prettiest girl in high school, was very popular, and always friendly with Scott; but she was his little sister's best friend, and maybe that had something to do with it. He and Penny had been friends ever since he moved to Edgemont two years ago, but for some reason he never got the nerve to ask her for a date at the right time—whenever that might have been. Maybe it was because he was too shy. He seldom asked any girls for a date even though he wanted to. He'd go to school dances and dance with all the girls and sometime he'd get the courage to ask some girl if he could walk them home.

Penny was never at the school dances because she had to work nearly every night and weekends behind the counter as a soda-jerk at the drug store soda fountain. It was the only establishment in town where kids could congregate and have a social life—other than at the pool hall. Scott would often drop in, sit on a stool at the fountain and talk with Penny, but she did not seem to pay much attention to him; sometimes it was as if her job making an ice cream cone for someone was more important than visiting with him.

Penny's father was a farmer who had been killed when a tractor tipped over on him; then her mother had to move to town and start a sewing shop to make a living. Penny had to help out, and they both worked to make ends meet.

Her working was not the biggest problem; however, it was that Penny was always going steady with some guy and it seemed to always be a guy with a car. The current boyfriend was Neil McCormick, a school dropout who worked at Igloo. He'd drive by the drug store with his car at ten o'clock when she got off work and drive her to her home that was in the outskirts of town. Scott felt he might be able to get her to go steady with him if he'd be there every night to walk her home, but it would be eleven o'clock and too late for him by the time he walked her home to the outskirts of town and got home himself, way past his curfew, and anyway, he never had access to his dad's car except for special occasions. On night of the prom, Penny would probably either be working at the soda fountain or going steady with some guy and not available as a date.

It was Saturday night and with nothing else to do, he walked down town to the drug store and climbed on a stool. "Hi, Penny, it seems like a quiet night; I suppose every one might be home studying, ha, ha." he said as a joke.

"Yeah Scott, you don't really believe anyone is busy studying at this hour on a Saturday night, do you? More than likely all the guys are at the pool hall and the girls are home listening to phonograph records and wishing they had a date to go dancing at the Pines. Why aren't you at the pool hall, I'll bet you are headed there?"

"No Penny, I saw the Soda Fountain was empty, so I dropped in to say hello and keep you company". He was hoping that would lead her to start a conversation, but she never seemed to pick up on that sort of opening. Just then, two sophomore girls who were her classmates walked in and sat in the first booth. Penny walked back to take their orders, which were banana splits, and she returned to behind the counter and busied herself filling the silver trays with double scoops of vanilla and chocolate ice cream, a banana, and a topping of chocolate sauce.

"Wow, banana splits," he remarked. "I love them, and you always make them extra special."

"Yeah, I do my best," she replied as she finished pouring on the chocolate sauce. Then she carried the trays back to the girls in the booth and stood visiting with them and engaging in a lot of laugher. She seemed to show little interest in returning to the counter for a further visit with Scott. Maybe he should wait a little longer until she finished with her customers; then ask her if he could have a date with her for the prom. He really wanted to take her to the prom—it would be their first official date, but he feared she would probably say "no." Rumors suggested she was now dating Neil McCormick, but Scott didn't think so and, anyway, she was not really going steady. He waited another ten minutes sitting on the stool as she gabbed with the girls in the booth. After five more minutes of sitting alone, he grew impatient, finished his coke and left.

Of course, Kelly was another possibility, but she was too moody and he did not understand her. She was a senior and very pretty and not going steady with anyone, but he had some apprehension about trying to date her again. She was so unpredictable. Last year at a school dance he asked her if he could walk her home and she said yes. They walked home holding hands and had a great time talking about all sort of things they both liked. The night ended with a warm kiss and date to go bike riding the next afternoon. The bike ride was a disaster. She suddenly threw a temper tantrum and rode away leaving him alone and in shock. Scott could not figure her out, but knew she was not someone he wanted for a prom date.

There were a couple other possibilities. Wanda was nice and very friendly, but not particularly attractive. Her family lived on a sheep farm five miles out in the country and she looked a lot like her mother who wore long shaggy hair, was dumpy, and never kept herself looking good; in another ten years that would be Wanda.

Then there were Ethel and Shirley. Both of them were nice, but a guy had to risk his reputation to date either of them. Shirley was the smartest girl in the junior class and fairly attractive with a great figure, but her dad worked as a card dealer in an illegal backroom in Buzz Beiber's Western Saloon. Ethel was also attractive with a slim waist and great bosom, but her mother worked as a barmaid of questionable reputation in Hank

Gordon's saloon. If Scott were to bring them home to meet his parents, he would have a lot of explaining to do with his father who ran the local bank. Edgemont was a small town and businessmen's reputations were important, whether that was right or wrong.

So, with the choices limited, it finally came down to asking Rosie for a date to the prom. Scott was pretty sure no one else had yet asked her, so he would not be embarrassed by getting a turn-down.

"Rosie, I've really be looking forward to the prom. I know this is early, but Rosie, I'd like to ask you if I could get a date with you for the prom."

"Oh Scott, I'd love to be your date for the prom," she gushed, and her face lighted up in a huge smile. "You and I will have a great time together."

There, the deed was done. It was still a month away, but Scot had a date; he could relax. Now he hoped Rosie and he would not have to act like they were going steady together—or whatever. He had never had an advance date with any girl and did not know what to expect from her, or how to act when they met in the school halls or sat in desks next to each other in the American History class. He thought she may want to go steady with him, but he offered no opening or encouragement. Even though she was fun to be around, Rosie did not hold a romantic attraction for him.

"Scott, do you have a date yet for the prom," asked his sister, Betty. "I know my best friend Penny is only a sophomore, but she is hoping you'll ask her. Penny is a really nice girl and even though it might look like she is going steady with Neil McCormick, she is not. He only drives her home so she won't have to walk that dark lonely road to her place. Why don't you ask her for a date to the prom?"

"Too late, Betty, I've already asked Rosie."

"Rosie! Oh no, Scott, why did you do that?" Then she paused. "Well, at least you will make Rosie happy. Everyone knows she has a crush on you." Damn! Why didn't he ask Penny when he still had a chance? It was too late now to back out of the date with Rosie.

The night for the prom arrived. It would be in the basement of the Methodist Church that had enough room for the dinner tables with plenty of extra room alongside for dancing. Music would be from phonograph records, and Glenn Miller and Tommy Dorsey were the favorites scheduled to be played. The girls in the junior and senior class together with the prom committee had spent the entire day Friday moving in the tables, decorating them and hanging multi-colored crape paper from the ceiling around the entry door and all the windows. The Methodist ladies were charging $1.75 a plate for a chicken dinner with all the trimmings and a dessert.

Scott's Dad had loaned him the family car for the evening. As he handed Scott the keys, his dad admonished him: "Now remember Scott, you are a gentleman, so remember to act like one."

"Yes, Dad," Scott muttered—whatever that was supposed to mean?

He picked up the corsage and the bottineau he ordered at the variety store that was the local broker for flowers. The town depended on a florist in Omaha for flowers and they arrived fresh on the 6 pm train from Alliance. The corsage was pink shattered carnations to go with the blue chiffon gown Rosie told him she was going to wear. The corsage cost him $1.25 and the flower for his lapel another $.35. All together with the $1.75 for his dinner and another $1.75 for Rosie's, the evening would cost him $5.10, which was more than twice as much as he earned in a day of digging ditch last summer with pick and shovel in Edgemont gumbo. If she wanted to stop at the drug store soda fountain on the way home to get a sundae and a coke, then it would cost probably a dollar more. Going on a date was expensive and he wondered how other guys could go steady with girls all the time and afford to do it.

He drove to the Montgomery's where Rosie lived with her married sister's family to pick her up. He was invited in by Rosie's brother-in-law Jim, and was invited to sit on the sofa and visit because Rosie was not quite ready. After a few minutes her sister, came into the room to say hello and inform Scott Rosie was almost ready, and also she was very excited and nervous.

Finally, Rosie made her appearance. She looked lovely with her hair freshly curled falling to her shoulders and wearing a blue chiffon gown that hung to the floor. She wore a pearl necklace and matching ear rings. She did look very attractive. Scott arose from the sofa, saying "hello", and walking over to where she stood. What was he supposed to do or say?

"Rosie, you look absolutely gorgeous, and that is a beautiful blue gown, and I like your hair that way. I brought you a corsage, and here, let me pin it on." With that he pulled the corsage out of a sack and lifted it to her chest where he attempted to pin it, not sure of the procedure. Her breasts pushed the gown out sharply in front, and he became all thumbs and very nervous when working near that area; he wasn't used to doing that sort of thing; and finally she helped him pick the spot where he could attach it onto the gown with the long pin provided. Then he handed her the red carnation bottineau and asked her to pin it on the label of his suit jacket. She seemed thrilled with all the activities. It was exciting for her and also a big event for Scott, his first formal date for a dinner and evening of dancing with a girl.

The prom unfolded exactly as planned. Before the dinner there was a short performance by six sophomores, three guys and three girls, who wore costumes and performed the Mexican Hat Dance, in keeping with the theme for the evening. They were the most popular sophomores from their class and voted on by the prom committee. It was considered a high honor for them to be chosen, and they had rehearsed the dance during the prior week. Then everyone sat down and Reverend Walker had been invited to attend and give the prayer. Dinner was served by the Methodist ladies.

It was a fun night, a good dance, and everyone had a great time. At the start of the evening, even before dinner was completed, the girls mingled with dance programs to entice their favorite guys to sign their program for one or more dances with them. Scott signed up for three dances with Rosie spaced through the evening plus the final dance, then a dance with each of the other girls at the prom.

To his surprise, Penny was there as the date of Gene Martin. Even though she was only a sophomore and Gene was a senior. It was the first time they had ever dated to his knowledge. What was she doing going to the prom with a senior? Now Scott was upset that he had not asked her for a date before asking Rosie; maybe she would have said yes and gone with him. He was jealous of Gene. Penny brought her dance card over to him and with a friendly smile insisted he sign up for three dances with her.

After the prom dance ended, everyone left the Methodist Hall, and most of them had rides. Rosie and Scott climbed in his father's car. He did not know the procedure of what to do on a date after a dance since he'd never had a date with a car before, but the talk among the guys in the locker room was that most of them drove up to reservoir hill to neck. He didn't know if Rosie would go for that.

"Rosie, what should we do now? Should we drive around for a while, and maybe we can go up to reservoir hill and see the view from up there; I hear the town lights are beautiful on a clear night like this?"

"Oh yes, Scott, let's do that," she responded eagerly. So he drove through the main part of town, through a few side streets, and then turned onto the dirt road that led up the hill where the town reservoir was located. Two other cars were parked in the dark with their lights turned off. He recognized Joe Gilmore's car, and he would be there with Vera. He drove beyond them a hundred yards and pulled off the road and parked where there seemed to be a good view of the lights of the town. She moved closer to him and then virtually fell into his arms. He kissed her and liked it, and she responded warmly, and he kissed her again and embraced her tightly. It was a cold night outside and the windshield was quickly steamed over. Then after a while she released her embrace of him and sat back on her side of the front seat.

"Oh Scott, wasn't that such a wonderful prom. I had such a great time with you. You are such a great person." How should he respond to that? It was a great prom and an okay night, but he wasn't overly thrilled like she seemed to be. He'd never been to a prom before. He had no intention of letting this conversation lead to another series of dates or going steady.

"Yes, Rosie, it certainly was a wonderful prom and I had a great time dancing with you and all the other girls—especially with you. You are such a good dancer. Where did you learn to dance like that?"

"Oh, Scott, peshaw, you don't really mean that. I learned at country dances down in Ardmore, but no one there ever danced fancy. So I just learned to dance the same way as all the other girls." Then she sat back on her side of the front seat and it was apparent she wanted to talk some more. She speculated about who the kids were parked in the other cars on Reservoirs Hill, and where all the other kids went after the dance, and who might be with whom. He went along with her and attempted to carry on a conversation. He wondered where Gene Martin and Penny were, if they were parked somewhere, and what they were doing. After a while Rosie said it might be getting late and maybe they should head for home so her sister would not be worried.

He drove her home and parked the car in front. He walked her to the door and kissed her. It had been a successful night. He had gone to the prom and survived his first real date.

THE WAR IS OVER

The war ended two weeks after dropping the two atomic bombs on Japan; it happened so quickly it left Americans in disbelief. The war had gone from Kamikazes diving planes into American ships, fierce fighting on Okinawa, and suddenly the unconditional surrender of Japanese forces, and peace. Peace—what was that? Scott had been in grade school in Buffalo Gap the last time there was peace. It had been too long in coming. After four years of continual war in Europe and the Pacific, how would Americans adjust? Scott had spent most of his high school years during wartime.

"I wonder when Denis and Edwin will be coming home?" asked his Mother on hearing the news of the Japanese surrender. "I remember after the Armistice was signed in 1918 that ended World War One, it took quite some time to bring the boys home. My brother Claude had to remain in France for a full year, and Clarence in Germany for nearly two years. I wonder if it will take that long after this war."

"Ethel, I don't think so," responded Scott's dad. "The government just announced a policy to prevent that sort of thing. It is called the point system. Every GI gets one point for each month of service, one additional point for each month overseas, additional points for serving in a combat zone, wounds received, and number of decorations. The points they have earned will determine when they get shipped home and discharged. They will need eighty points for discharge and it may drop to sixty points shortly. It seems like a fair system."

"When does that mean Denis and Edwin will be discharged?" she asked.

"Well, Denis has been in for three years, at sea for two, and most of that time in a combat zone, so he must already have his eighty points and in line for discharge.

"That is great news," she replied. "I'll bet he will be ready to get home. I wonder what his plans are. There are no jobs available anywhere, so maybe he'll go to college."

In fact, over a million GIs faced the same question: what to do? The defense industry had immediately shut down all the armament factories at the war's end, and the fate of the Black Hills Ordnance Depot at Igloo was even in question. At least there was no new hiring and some workers were already being laid off.

When Denis was discharged in a couple months and returned home, he did what virtually all other GIs did; they joined what they called the 52/20 club, which meant collecting an unemployment check of $20 per week for 52 weeks. Edwin returned home six months later. In the fall they both returned to college utilizing the GI Bill at the South Dakota School of Mines in Rapid City.

There was no job available for Scott when he completed his senior year and graduated from high school. The previous summer he had worked a seventy hour week at Igloo and earned a paycheck each week of $125; now he faced the prospect of no job and no paycheck. It did not leave him in desperate straits because just prior to graduation he was notified that he had been selected to receive a coveted NROTC scholarship that provided for a fully-paid education at the University of Colorado. He could just sit at home all summer and read cowboy short stories in the *Saturday Evening Post* magazine. After a week of doing that and getting somewhat bored, he heard the phone ring one morning.

"Hello", he answered.

"Scott, Dad,"

"Yes Dad, why are you calling?"

'I was talking on the phone to our Buffalo Gap branch bank this morning when Rudolph Schroth walked in. You remember him from when we lived there. He runs the 7/11 ranch and is a good customer of the bank. Well, I asked Carp to hand the phone to Rudolph so I could say hello, and while I was talking to him I asked about a job for you this summer on the ranch. He said, sure come over next week and he'd put you to work. He said the pay for his ranch hands is only one dollar a day plus room and board. He said that's all he could afford under the circumstances. Scott, I know it isn't much for wages, but how does that sound to you?"

"Well," Scott responded after a moment of silence. "It a drop in pay of over a hundred and twenty dollars a week from my job at Igloo, but I guess I don't have much other chance of getting any work. Besides being a cowboy on the 7/11 ranch might be okay. I hear Dick Sewright and Don Eibert from the Hot Springs football team are already working there and they are good friends of mine, so it might be fun." Then he hesitated for a moment. "Yeah, Dad, I think that sounds okay. Next week I'll become a Buffalo Gap cowboy again.

When he arrived at the ranch the following Monday, he was put to work by the foreman, Tom Judd, who he already knew. Tom's daughter, Herberta, had been a classmate of his one year in the Buffalo Gap elementary school, but that previous acquaintance with Tom cut no ice; he had to start at the bottom of the totem pole among all the ranch hands. His first job was shoveling manure from the horse barn into a manure spreader and driving a team of work horses pulling the wagon out to the fields and spreading the manure as fertilizer. It was below the dignity of most other cowboys, but Scott found it was easier than his next job that was working atop a haystack with pitch fork spreading hay to all the four corners. He was hoping in a week or two he might be promoted into a saddle.

Cowboy was hard work, but he came to love it, and also the camaraderie of living with a half dozen ranch hands. They each had a cot around the perimeter of the bunk house, and located in the center between all of them was a pool table. The foreman, Tom Judd, loved to play pool so he had purchased the pool table when it came up for sale at Frenchie's saloon in Buffalo Gap. On rainy days when work was not possible out in the fields, Tom would permit the hands to stay in the bunk house and he challenged them to pool. At long-last, the expertise Scott had developed in Nate-the-Barber's pool hall became an asset. He had become an excellent pool shot back then and was now able to beat the foreman in a game of twenty-call-shot; however, he was smart enough to stay close in the score, but always let Tom win the final game. Losing a game of pool to the foreman was better than riding a horse in a cold rainstorm.

His favorite times were in the saddle as they rode up the high mountains to the south and rounded up the cattle on the high plateau. It was a beautiful area, and the plateau fell off to the east in the headwaters of Calico Canyon and Knapp Canyon that he had climbed from the mouth of the canyons with his sister and brother, Betty and Billy, when they lived in Buffalo Gap. Now he had explored this remote area from the mouths of the canyons up to their headwaters.

The summer came to an end. Scott left the 7/11 ranch to return home to Edgemont briefly, and then packed for college. He was ready to leave his teenage years behind, was now on the threshold of college, and he had no intention of looking back at those troubled years in high school. What adventures lay ahead? He couldn't wait to find out.

POST-SCRIPT

When I wrote this book, which is 95% autobiographical, I decided to call it a novel and use a fictional name to allow me to embellish and add a bit more color and drama to that period in my life in high school that seemed (at the time) to lack those qualities.

Psychologists tell us that in the twilight Golden Years (where I now find myself at the age of eighty-five) when we close our eyes and dream, we are often carried back to that period we found most pleasant and satisfying. For me, the time often in my musings is during the years related in my previous novel, *RIDING MY HORSE: Growing Up in Buffalo Gap*. Even though it took place during the abject poverty of the 1930s Great Depression, those were relatively carefree days when as a child my real, genuine responsibilities were essentially zilch. They were happy times of my youth, and I think about them often.

By contrast, I seldom spend time dreaming or contemplating the times of high school reflected in this novel. I don't know why? Was it because they were the war years—or being a teenager? No Matter. Perhaps during that period (and maybe other people's lives as well) in high school we faced for the first time the harsh realities of "true life".

Buffalo Gap summons sweet dreams: Edgemont seldom does.

A song still embedded in my memory from that era is *When Day is Done*, a hit by Bing Crosby he sang on his weekly radio show.

When day is done and shadows fall, I dream of you
When day is done . . . I think of all the joys we knew . . .

It was the song our Senior Sextet in cap and gown sang on graduation night: Wilbur Wacker, Chub Bergen, Johnny Gallegos, Freddie Guynn, Chuck Johnson, and me. Our classmate, Arlene Roselius, strummed the keys of the piano alongside; she provided rather loud accompaniment because of our tendency to sing off-key. Wilbur Wacker was an excellent singer from his training at the Gospel Tabernacle Church, and he carried our group in song; the rest of us took his lead standing close, and lip-synched.

That was seventy years ago and I can recall it like it was yesterday. Now I realize why that song was chosen for our graduation ceremony (other than it was the hit song of the day). It was a nostalgic and emotional remembrance for that night and time in our lives.

When day is done and shadows fall, we *dream of all the joys we knew*. In my musings, I often return to live again those wonderful days.